Deceived

Patricia H. Rushford

Jennie McGrady Mystery Series

1. *Too Many Secrets*
2. *Silent Witness*
3. *Pursued*
4. *Deceived*

Deceived

Patricia H. Rushford

BETHANY HOUSE PUBLISHERS
MINNEAPOLIS, MINNESOTA 55438

DECEIVED
Patricia Rushford

Cover illustration by Andrea Jorgenson

Coke is a registered trademark of the Coca-Cola Corporation.
Jacuzzi is a registered trademark of
Jacuzzi Brothers, Jacuzzi Inc.
Kleenex is a registered trademark of Kimberly-Clark.
Styrofoam is a registered trademark of Dow Plastics.

Library of Congress Catalog Card Number 94–33038

ISBN 1–55661–334–2

Published by Bethany House Publishers
A Ministry of Bethany Fellowship, Inc.
11300 Hampshire Avenue South,
Minneapolis, Minnesota 55438

Printed in the United States of America

Dedicated to

Ryan, Scott, Jason, and Jerry
and to Tony and Davin

PATRICIA RUSHFORD is an award-winning writer, speaker, and teacher who has published almost twenty books and numerous articles, including *What Kids Need Most in a Mom, The Humpty Dumpty Syndrome: Putting Yourself Back Together Again*, and her first young adult novel, *Kristen's Choice*. She is a registered nurse and has a master's degree in counseling from Western Evangelical Seminary. She and her husband, Ron, live in Washington State and have two grown children, six grandchildren, and lots of nephews and nieces.

1

Jennie McGrady walked along a deserted wharf. She had no idea how she'd gotten there. Jennie only knew that she'd gone to meet her father, Jason McGrady, who had been missing for five years. Her leather-soled shoes made a faint scraping sound against the wooden planks. She stopped in a halo of light near a fishing boat. A chilling mist swirled around her.

Jennie stuffed her hands in the pockets of her jacket. A car door slammed in the distance. She listened for footsteps, but heard only the sound of water lapping against the pilings. A tall bulky form emerged from the shadows. The man wore a hat and trench coat and a Humphrey Bogart mask. Jennie backed away. "W-who are you?" she stammered.

"Your father. You wanted to see me."

"No," she whispered, fear gripping her in icy tentacles. "I . . . I mean, yes, but you're not . . ."

The man reached up and pulled at the mask, distorting its features. Hollow black eyes slimed into a deformed nose. Like a rubber band it broke away from his face and snapped against his hand.

Jennie took another step back. Her gaze shifted from the mask to his face.

Her father smiled. "Hello, Jennie." His eyes looked black in the dim light.

"Dad?" Her fears vanished.

He lifted his arms in welcome and Jennie ran into them. "I knew you'd come." When he didn't respond, she drew back to study him. The man in her arms was no longer her father.

Jennie screamed and wrenched out of his grasp. The stranger, face distorted now with pain, dropped his arms to his side and walked away.

———————

Jennie waited for the red light on Front Street to change. The frightening dream drifted in and out of her mind like an outgoing tide. She tried to grasp it again and hold on to its meaning. Not all of it, of course, but the part about Dad being alive. That was what had motivated her to come this far. Dad was alive. That was what she needed to remember.

Jennie drove another two blocks, then pulled into the parking lot near Portland's new glass-domed skyscraper. She'd changed her mind a dozen times that morning— almost as many times as she'd changed her clothes.

The colorful new crinkle skirt, hot pink top, and black crocheted vest seemed like a good choice, but what did she know? For the first time in ages she hadn't asked her cousin and best friend, Lisa, to advise her. Unfortunately, she couldn't risk letting Lisa or anyone else in the family know what she was about to do.

Stepping out of her white Mustang, Jennie glanced up at the twenty-story building and gave herself another pep talk. *You have to do this, McGrady. It may be the last chance you'll ever have to find Dad.*

True, her more cautious side agreed, *but Mom's going to kill you when she finds out.*

Ignoring the protesting voices in her head, Jennie grabbed her black leather backpack and, after turning in her keys and collecting a ticket from the parking lot attendant, merged into the foot traffic on the crowded sidewalk. She hauled in a deep breath and crossed the street. The stench of exhaust fumes and the aroma of fresh bread competed for space in the warm spring air.

The immense marble foyer of the KKNG Building looked cold and intimidating. A small glassed-in cage at the far right of the elevators held a receptionist captive. According to the instructions Jennie had been given, her name would be on the receptionist's security list. "Just introduce yourself," the man had said, "and they'll let you in."

She swallowed hard. A warning voice that sounded a lot like Mom haunted her. *Don't do it, Jennie. You're making a terrible mistake.*

For months her mother had been saying, "It's time to stop living in the past. Your father is dead. We all need to accept that fact and get on with our lives." Mom had gotten on with her life all right. Boyfriend and all.

Jennie ignored the nagging voices and straightened to her full five foot ten inches. McGrady stubbornness propelled her forward. She had no intention of giving up. Especially not when she had the proof she needed in her backpack.

"Can I help you?" The receptionist, whose name badge read *Charlotte*, looked up and smiled. Her cute little nose, blond hair, and yellow suit reminded Jennie of Woodstock, Snoopy's bird friend in the Charlie Brown comic strip. She didn't seem to mind being locked up in the glass cage. Jennie felt claustrophobic just thinking about it.

"Hi. I'm Jennie McGrady. I have an appointment with John Hendricks."

"McGrady," Charlotte murmured as she scanned the list of names. "Oh, right. You're here to tape a segment for *Missing in America*. That's such an incredible show. Did you see it last week when the lady from New Mexico was reunited with her husband? I still get misty-eyed over it. I mean . . . just think about it. He'd been missing for fourteen years."

Jennie nodded. The show had revived her hopes. She had called the producer the next day and told him about her father. He was so impressed he asked her to come to the local affiliate station, KKNG-TV, to tape an interview. "That's why I called. I thought maybe—"

"Your husband is missing?" Charlotte interrupted. "You don't look old enough to have a husband."

"No." Jennie paused, wishing Charlotte would stop twittering and just let her in. If she thought too much about what she was going to do, she'd change her mind again. "It's my father."

"Oh." Charlotte scrunched her face up in an empathetic frown. "You poor thing. I hope you find him." She lifted a clipboard from her desk and handed it to Jennie. "We need you to sign a release form."

Jennie glanced over the paper, ignored the part where kids under eighteen needed parental permission, and signed her name. Okay, so she wasn't eighteen. What else could she do? Jennie swallowed back her niggling conscience and handed the clipboard back to Charlotte.

"Have a seat in the reception area and I'll call Mr. Hendricks." The receptionist pointed through a window to a love seat and two chairs positioned on a plush mauve carpet near a wide-screen television set.

The door to Jennie's right buzzed and she pushed it open. Charlotte flashed her a smile and chirped, "Good luck with the taping," then turned to answer the phone.

Jennie sank into the floral-print chair facing the stairs. The two o'clock soap opera was just coming on and Jennie wished she had a remote control so she could click it off. She hated soaps. Partly because they were depressing and partly because she didn't want to be reminded of her own dismal love life.

The guy on screen was a tall, blond, blue-eyed hunk who looked a little too much like her boyfriend, Ryan Johnson. Jennie turned her gaze from the television set to the stairs, but Ryan's image lingered in her mind. Thinking about Ryan used to be fun. These days it saddened her. Ryan was still in Alaska working on a fishing boat and probably would be all summer. Before he left, they'd moved from being good friends into something more. . . . Jennie almost laughed aloud at the word that popped into her head. *Intimate?* Hardly. She hadn't seen him for so long she had no idea how she felt—or worse, how Ryan felt.

"You must be Jennie." A man's deep voice interrupted her thoughts. A guy in his midthirties wearing round wire-rimmed glasses and a business suit appeared at the top of the stairs. "Hi. I'm John Hendricks. Welcome." He reached a hand toward her as he approached. Jennie stood and shook it, trying to act as if she taped television interviews every day.

Being at eye level with him helped, but not much. She opened her mouth hoping something intelligent would come out, but nothing did.

"You're nervous," Hendricks grinned at her. His glasses slipped forward. He pushed them back and kept talking without missing a beat. "Most people are. Being on television can be unnerving, but once you get into your story, the butterflies will quiet down."

Jennie nodded. "I hope so." She followed him down a winding staircase, along a maze of hallways, and through a door with a sign that read CAUTION—DO NOT ENTER WHILE RED LIGHT IS BLINKING. The red light was blinking. They went in anyway. A cavernous, charcoal gray room swallowed them. A dozen or so people roamed around laughing, talking, and drinking out of Styrofoam cups.

"Great. You're here. Just in time." A tiny dark-haired woman in tight black jeans, a white silk shirt, black leather vest, and a headset appeared at Jennie's side and gave her a quick, firm handshake.

"This is Toni Baker," Hendricks said. "She'll be producing the segment for us. Toni's the best in the business. All we need to do is follow orders and we'll have a great program."

"Okay, guys, get the lead out," Toni barked at a group of people gathered around an industrial-sized coffeepot. "We've got a show to do." Turning back to Hendricks she said, "Take Jennie up to the set. Get a mike on her and fill her in." She looked down at the clipboard and back at Jennie. "Pictures. You got the pictures you want us to show?"

Jennie nodded and unzipped her pack. She pulled out the large, framed picture of her dad and handed it to Toni. Then from a small envelope, Jennie drew out the photo she'd gotten in the mail from Debbie Cole.

Dad's longtime friend from Florida had recently sent

Jennie some old photos of their college days. But as Jennie soon discovered, they weren't all old. Because of the full beard and mustache she hadn't recognized him. In the photo, Dad's arms were draped around Debbie and Ken Cole. Jennie could still feel the goose bumps from the moment when she'd turned the photo over and read *Jason, Debbie, and Ken—Fort Myers Beach 7/7/88*—two months after Dad's disappearance. Hesitantly, she handed the photo to Toni.

As if reading Jennie's mind, Toni gave her a reassuring smile. "Don't worry. We'll take good care of them."

"Let's get you wired," Hendricks said as he led Jennie toward the set.

"I think I already am," Jennie muttered, following him through the obstacle course of cameras and cables.

Hendricks chuckled. "You'll do fine. Just relax and talk to me. Ignore the cameras and be yourself."

A stagehand appeared behind her as she sat down in one of the two chairs angled to look like a cozy living room. He clipped a tiny microphone to her vest, tucked the wire under her arm, and hid it behind her.

Three huge television cameras stood guard. Ignoring them would be like trying to eat a banana with an 800-pound gorilla watching. Jennie took several deep breaths and tried not to think about the fact that in a little over a week her story, and a plea to her father or anyone who might have seen him, would be broadcast to millions of people across the country.

"Don't I need makeup or something?" she asked.

"No . . ." Hendricks paused and scrutinized her face. "What you have on is perfect. Unless you'd be more comfortable."

She shrugged, feeling relieved. Jennie never wore

15

much makeup—didn't need to. She had dark blue eyes and long dark lashes. Mascara would have made her look overdone, like Cleopatra. She had touched up her cheeks with a brushstroke of blush and rubbed it until the edges disappeared. Normally she didn't need blush either, but the nightmare had left her pale and shaken.

Her already taut nerves tightened with Toni's countdown: "Five-four-three-two-one. Hit it!"

Jennie eased out the breath she'd been holding and turned to face John Hendricks.

"Five years ago," Hendricks began, "Jason McGrady disappeared without a trace. McGrady, we've learned, was a federal agent, working covert operations with both the FBI and the DEA—the Drug Enforcement Administration. Authorities say his plane went down in the icy waters of Puget Sound, near Seattle, during a storm. Lost at sea? Perhaps.

"His daughter, Jennie, however, has another theory, and we'll be hearing her side of this mysterious disappearance today.

"Jennie," he said, turning toward her, "tell us why you're so certain your father is still alive."

Twenty minutes later the interview ended and Jennie couldn't believe how easy it had been or how quickly the time had gone.

"You did a wonderful job, Jennie," Hendricks told her. "If your father is out there, he'll know you're looking for him. And I've got to admit, stories like yours make my job as a reporter challenging. In fact, I'm hoping to follow up on this one myself."

Toni handed her the precious photos and added, "We'll Express Mail the tape to the head office in Los Angeles today and let you know when they plan to air it.

It will probably be a week or so."

Jennie left the building feeling relieved that the program had gone so well. The butterflies had vanished, but in their place a tight band of uneasiness wound itself around her chest.

She hated deceiving her family, especially Gram. But what else could she do? Gram and her FBI friend Jason Bradley had promised to help Jennie find Dad—which was great because, like her father, J.B. had ties with both the FBI and the DEA. The next thing Jennie knew, J.B. had whisked Gram off to Europe. An assignment, he'd said. Some assignment.

When they returned home, Jennie showed them the photo she'd received from Debbie. The next day Gram and J.B. told her that Debbie admitted she may have made a mistake and written down the wrong year, and that she couldn't even be certain the man in the photo was Jason McGrady. Then they *ordered* Jennie to stop trying to find Dad. Gram had totally changed her mind. And that wasn't all she'd changed.

For one thing, her name was no longer McGrady, but Bradley. Mrs. Jason Bradley. The memory still burned in Jennie's mind.

"I know you want to find your father, dear," Gram had said. "I'd like nothing more than to have my son home again." Tears filled Gram's faded cobalt eyes. "But we both have to learn to set aside our dreams and accept reality. Your father is gone and he's never coming back."

Jennie had been furious at first. Without Gram's police training and contacts with federal agencies, finding Dad would have been almost impossible. Almost. Thanks to *Missing in America*, Jennie had another option. Despite all the efforts of her family to dissuade her, Jennie held firm to her conviction. Dad was out there somewhere and she intended to prove it. As she'd reminded her mother dozens of times, "There's a big difference between being dead and being presumed dead."

2

"Jennie McGrady, that has got to be the craziest stunt you've ever pulled." Lisa jabbed a straw into her Coke. "When Gram and your mom find out they're going to kill you."

Jennie winced and leaned back in her chair. "I had to do something. I know Dad's alive. I don't care what anyone says."

"But why television?" Lisa asked. "Why couldn't you have just run an ad in the paper, or written to Ann Landers?"

"Going on TV was the best way. Maybe he'll see me on the show and recognize his pictures, like that man who was on last week. Or maybe someone else will recognize him. I'm not sorry I did it, we just can't let anyone in our family watch the program tonight."

Lisa leaned forward, resting her arms on the table. "Why did you have to pick *Missing in America*? It's one of the most popular television programs in the country. Never mind that it's Gram's favorite. She never misses it."

"I know, but it's out of my hands now. The station called this afternoon and said they're airing it tonight. We just have to keep the family busy from eight to nine."

Lisa pulled on a strand of her copper-colored curls

and wove it around her fingers. "Do you realize what this could do to us?"

"What do you mean?"

"The cruise. I can't believe you didn't think about it. If your mom finds out she'll never let you go. And if I help you, I won't be able to go either."

The cruise was Lisa's sixteenth birthday present from Gram. Gram had taken Jennie to Florida only a couple of weeks earlier for her birthday. Since Gram and J.B. had gotten married, they decided to buy two more tickets—one for J.B. so he and Gram could enjoy a honeymoon and one for Jennie so Lisa would have a companion.

"You're wrong. I did think about the cruise. I know how important it is to you. When I called in to ask about being on the show, they told me they'd tape the interview on Friday and air it in a couple weeks. I figured we'd be back by then and it wouldn't matter. Dad would see it and hopefully come home." She closed her eyes and bit her lip. When she said it out loud it sounded crazy.

"So what went wrong?"

"Nothing. It went really well—too well. The producer loved the show and decided to broadcast it right away."

"I hate it when you drag me into your nutty schemes. But I guess I can understand why you did it. I just hope it's worth it, Jennie. I hope your dad is alive and sees it and contacts you."

"Me too." Jennie picked up her damp napkin and tore it in half. "So you'll help me?"

"Do I have a choice?"

"Yes." She tore the two halves into fourths. "I'm sorry. I shouldn't have dragged you into this. Never mind. I'll handle it."

Lisa sighed. "No. I'll help. I guess I owe you that much for helping Allison."

Allison, one of the Rose Festival Princesses, was a good friend of Lisa's. A shudder ran through Jennie as she remembered the gory details. She'd misjudged one of the players in a deadly game and had nearly gotten herself and Lisa killed.

Jennie pushed the images from her mind, concentrating instead on the task at hand. "Good," she said. "I was thinking maybe we could invite everyone out for pizza and offer to pay."

"We?" Lisa pushed her chair back and slipped the straps of her bag onto her shoulder. "I don't think so, Jennie. I don't owe you that much. I'll help, but no way am I going to pick up the tab."

"Okay, okay. I'll dip into the money Mr. Beaumont gave me for helping the police track down Allison's stalker."

"Wait," Lisa interrupted. "Maybe neither of us will have to buy. I've got another idea. First, I need to talk to my mom. Gram and J.B. will be at our house for dinner. I'll see if you guys can come too. She's having pot roast. I could switch off the circuit breaker for a couple of hours so we'd have to eat late."

Jennie shook her head. "Too complicated. Besides, we need to get them out of the house. With my luck Gram would suggest eating in the living room. Why couldn't we just find something to celebrate and take everyone out for pizza? Then maybe we could suggest a movie."

"Hmmm. You check that out. I'll call you when I find out what everyone's doing."

Lisa hurried off, leaving nothing behind but the exotic scent of the hundred-dollar-an-ounce perfume she'd sampled in Nordstrom's. Jennie smiled and finished off her drink. Lisa loved the perfume, but on her allowance she could only afford an occasional whiff. Whenever they went shopping, Lisa sprayed a little on whatever outfit she was wearing.

Jennie cleared off their table and headed for the parking lot. They usually drove places together, but Jennie needed to pick up her mom, who'd been working with a client at the airport. Besides, now that Lisa had her driver's license, she looked for any excuse whatsoever to take her own car.

During the drive, Jennie puzzled over the changes that had taken place in her mother over the past few months. It began, of course, with Mom's engagement to Michael Rhodes. Jennie would never forget the day Michael showed up on their doorstep to help celebrate Nick's fifth birthday. Her little brother still insisted God had sent him a daddy for his birthday.

Just thinking about it made her stomach churn. For a while Mom was so intent on marriage that Jennie feared Nick's wish would come true. Lately, though, Mom had backed off the marriage thing. "Michael's a little too much like your father," she'd said. "I just don't want another man who's more married to his work than to me."

In a way Jennie felt sorry for Michael. She was starting to like him—not as a stepfather, of course. As remote as the possibility seemed, Jennie still hoped her father would come home and that he and her mother would be able to work things out. Maybe Dad would try to stay home more. Maybe Mom would stop resenting his work.

Prior to his disappearance, Jason McGrady had worked for the government as a federal agent, like his father, Ian McGrady, and his father before that. Gram used to be a police officer, but after Grandpa Ian was killed, she retired from the force and decided to become a writer. Now she wrote articles for travel magazines, but still kept her connections with the FBI. Jennie intended to carry on the tradition. She planned to study law in college and, in the meantime, learn all she could about law enforcement from Gram.

And that was another change. Gram hardly seemed like Gram anymore. She'd come back from her trip to Europe all bubbly and excited about her new life with J.B.

Disappointed, angry, and hurt over Gram's refusal to search for Dad, Jennie had only half listened to Gram and J.B. tell the story of his proposal at the top of the Eiffel Tower and their makeshift wedding at the U.S. Embassy. Ordinarily it would have sounded romantic and exciting. But Jennie had felt numb.

Not even the invitation to join them on the cruise excited her. On the outside Jennie pretended to be grateful, but inside she couldn't feel much of anything except disappointment.

Jennie pulled up to the airport arrival area where Mom was to meet her. She felt like an actress trying out for her first major role. *Settle down, McGrady*, she told herself. *By the time Mom finds out, the interview and the pictures of Dad will already have aired on national television.*

Uneasiness settled around her like a dismal fog. *What if you've made a mistake, McGrady?* a voice in her head cautioned. *What if your dad is dead? Or worse, what if he's alive and doesn't want to be found?*

3

"It worked," Jennie murmured as she leaned toward her cousin.

"Of course." Lisa tossed some buttered popcorn into her mouth and offered Jennie some. "They loved the movie idea. Besides, my mom couldn't resist spending some time with me. She's been kind of nervous about my going on this cruise. It's like she's afraid I won't come back."

"I don't think she's afraid you won't come back," Jennie whispered. "I think she's afraid of what—or who—you'll come back with."

"What are you talking about?" Lisa frowned.

"Lisa, you've been telling everybody that you're going to meet the man of your dreams on this cruise. If I were your mother I'd be nervous too."

Lisa grinned, her green eyes reflecting the theater's subdued light. "Oh that. She knows I'm not serious." Lisa examined a kernel of popped corn before putting it in her mouth. "It would be exciting if I did meet him though, wouldn't it?"

"Who?"

"Mr. Right. The man of my dreams."

"I thought Brad was the man of your dreams." Jennie

slouched in her back-row seat trying to get comfortable.

"Not anymore. We broke up."

"You're kidding!" Jennie had the feeling the news was more upsetting to her than to Lisa. Either that or Lisa was hiding her hurt feelings awfully well. "What happened?"

"He dumped me for another woman."

"Oh, Lisa, that's terrible. I'm sorry."

"Don't be. I'm okay with it. Really."

"Okay with what, honey?" Aunt Kate plopped into the seat in front of Jennie and twisted around to look at Lisa.

"Nothing, Mom. I was just telling Jennie about Brad."

Before Aunt Kate could reply, Uncle Kevin, Mom, and Michael filed in and took the empty seats next to her. The lights dimmed.

Gram and J.B. entered the theater and took the seats on the end next to Jennie. She adored Gram, at least she had until a few days ago. Being married to J.B. had changed her so much, Jennie was beginning to wonder if Gram had been invaded by aliens.

Gram took hold of Jennie's hand and squeezed it. "I'm delighted you girls thought of this little outing. I haven't been to a movie in months."

Jennie smiled, hoping her face wouldn't betray the feelings stirring around inside. She couldn't ever remember being angry with Gram, but then Gram had never seemed so far away—or so totally against her.

The story was beautiful and sad. Between them, they must have gone through a full box of Kleenex. Fortunately, Aunt Kate had read the reviews and came prepared. When they left the theater they looked more like

a funeral party than a family out for an evening of entertainment.

"Let's pick up those new grandsons of mine and stop
at Ricardo's for dessert," J.B. suggested. "My treat." His
"new" grandsons were Nick, Jennie's little brother, and
Lisa's brother, Kurt. The boys had gone to Toyland, a
kind of short-term day-care where parents could leave
their kids while they went shopping or out for the evening.
Playing suited both boys much more than sitting still for
two hours.

"Want to?" Michael asked Mom.

"I don't want anything sweet, but I'll have some coffee
while the rest of you eat."

Mom was always on a diet, and Jennie couldn't resist
teasing her. "Don't believe a word she says, Michael.
Mom's known in dessert circles as Bite Woman. All she
ever orders is the silverware, but when it's all over she's
eaten more than all the rest of us combined."

Aunt Kate laughed and agreed. Mom stifled a grin
and pouted. Taking Michael's arm, she asked, "Are you
going to let them pick on me like that?"

"I don't know. Are you going to want a bite of my
New York cheesecake?"

"Bite Woman has retired," Mom said in a confident
tone, then paused. "Cheesecake?" The way she said it left
no room for doubt. Bite Woman was about to strike again.

Michael pulled her close and kissed her nose, as if to
let her know she could have all the bites she wanted. The
interaction between them created a fluttery sensation in
Jennie's stomach. They were acting like an engaged couple again. *Come on, Dad,* Jennie half pleaded and half
prayed. *Please come home soon. Time is running out.*

"Jennie . . ." Lisa tugged at her arm. "Are you coming?"

"Yeah."

Jennie and Lisa had driven together. Since they had room in the car, they offered to collect Nick and Kurt and meet the adults at Ricardo's. The adults piled into Uncle Kevin's van while Jennie and Lisa headed for the car.

When they were out of earshot, Jennie heaved a sigh of relief. "Thanks, Lisa. I owe you one."

"I know I should say forget it, but I won't." Lisa slid in behind the driver's seat of her parents' cranberry red Taurus while Jennie got into the passenger side.

"It still seems strange to have you driving."

"Get used to it. I plan to do a lot of it this summer." Lisa backed out of her parking place. A horn blared. She slammed on the brakes.

The force yanked Jennie against the seat belt. "Ouch. Not if you keep driving like that you won't."

"Would you relax? I didn't hit him. Besides, it was his fault. He shouldn't have been driving behind me when I was trying to back out. And he shouldn't be driving a black car."

"I can't believe you just said that." Jennie reached for the door. "I think I'll go ride in the van."

Lisa glanced at Jennie and chuckled. "Don't look so shocked. I'm just kidding."

"Driving is serious business." Jennie winced and groaned. "I can't believe *I* said that. I sounded just like my mother."

"It's okay, I forgive you." Lisa backed out again and then inched forward, nearly rear-ending the car ahead of her.

Jennie planted her feet on the floor and braced herself. She'd only ridden with Lisa a couple of times and was about ready to buy a crash helmet and a well-padded driving suit.

Lisa waved at a driver in a silver Honda, who stopped to let them onto the main road. After they'd gone a couple of blocks, Jennie began to relax. She leaned her head against the headrest and closed her eyes.

"Jennie?" Lisa's voice sounded strained.

Jennie straightened. "What's wrong?"

Lisa glanced in the rearview mirror. "Remember the guy who stopped to let us get in front of him at the theater?"

Jennie nodded.

"I think he's still following us."

Jennie lowered the visor on the passenger side and looked into the mirror, but all she could see was the blinding glare of headlights. "We've only gone a couple of miles. Maybe he just happens to be going in the same direction."

"You're probably right. It just makes me nervous when someone stays behind me like that."

"Me too. It might be a coincidence, but if he follows us into the parking lot at Toyland, I'm calling the police."

Adrenaline stirred in Jennie's blood. Another mystery? The idea excited her. When Lisa pulled into the parking lot the car zipped by. Jennie sighed. "False alarm," she said, feeling relieved and disappointed at the same time.

Even with promises of ice cream, it took ten minutes for Jennie and Lisa to pry their little brothers out of Toyland's tunnel maze. At the restaurant the girls split a chocolate fudge truffle cake drizzled with raspberry sauce. Decadent.

While she ate, Jennie glanced around at her family.

She could almost see the aura of love hovering around them. Only one thing marred their family portrait. Dad should have been sitting in Michael's place. She closed her eyes, trying to imagine it. Dad feeding Mom a piece of cheesecake, his eyes full of admiration. The man who appeared behind her closed eyelids, however, wasn't Jennie's father. It was Michael.

4

Jennie stumbled out of bed at seven the next morning, threw on her robe, and headed downstairs. The phone rang once. Mom picked it up in the kitchen.

"She what?" Mom yelled just as Jennie reached the dining room. After a long silence she spoke again. "I can't believe Jennie would do a thing like that. Are you sure?"

Panic slammed through Jennie's body with the impact of a cement truck. Who had seen the show and phoned? Pulling an about-face, she sneaked back up the stairs and into her room. Any second now, Mom would barge in and demand an explanation. Fifteen minutes went by. No Mom. Jennie got dressed and braided her hair. Still no Mom.

This was not good. Jennie thought about packing her clothes and escaping through her bedroom window when a car pulled into the driveway. Gram and J.B. Mom had called in reinforcements.

Unable to stand the suspense, Jennie emerged from her room and eased down the stairs. She'd either get nailed or find out what was going on. She watched from the landing as Mom let Gram and J.B. in. They each gave Mom a hug and purred condolences.

"What's going on?" Jennie asked innocently.

They glanced in her direction. J.B. looked annoyed, and Gram, disappointed. Mom stared through Jennie as if she were invisible. Mom's pasty complexion and red-rimmed eyes told Jennie she'd been crying.

Come on, guys, lighten up, she wanted to say. *So I went on television to try and find Dad. Is that so bad?* They were acting as if someone had died.

The silence crackled with unspoken charges—all leveled at Jennie.

J.B. cleared his throat. "I think we need to talk, lass."

Mom started for the living room, then stopped. "Would you like some coffee?" she asked and without waiting for their answers headed into the kitchen.

J.B. and Gram took a seat on the couch and asked Jennie to join them. Jennie loosened her hold on the bannister, now more puzzled than afraid. Why would Mom cut and run? Gram and J.B. seemed afraid of saying the wrong thing. Why didn't they just yell at her and get it over with? Unless . . . Jennie hurried down the rest of the stairs. "What's going on?" she asked. "Has someone been hurt?"

"Not in the way you mean." Gram pinched her lips together and glanced at J.B. as if she suddenly needed his support. That was strange. Gram was one of the most in-charge people Jennie knew. Now she seemed too upset to even talk. Jennie dropped into the chair next to the couch, taut as an overinflated balloon. One more second and she'd explode.

She jumped up and paced across the oriental rug, then stopped in front of them. "I don't understand what all the fuss is about. All I did was try to get some help to find Dad. You guys are acting like I committed murder or something. So I went on television and did a little interview. What's the big deal?" Jennie slumped back into her chair again. "How did you find out anyway?"

"I had a phone call waiting for me when I got home last night, lass. From Washington."

"Washington?" Jennie swallowed hard. "As in D.C.?"

"As in the FBI. Before the accident, your father had been loaned to the DEA for some undercover work. We were up until two this morning trying to work out some kind of damage control."

"I knew he was on a special assignment," Jennie said, "but that was five years ago. What's that got to do with finding him now?"

"A great deal, I'm afraid. They are not happy, lass. Unfortunately, you didn't just appear on television. You interfered with national security. Your interview has investigative reporters from all over the country storming the intelligence agencies in Washington."

"I don't understand."

Gram leaned forward. "You've opened a Pandora's box, dear. The press loves to get hold of stories like this. They think the government is hiding something."

"By playing on public sympathy," J.B. added, "you've managed to make both agencies look like they're whitewashing a terrible crime."

"I . . . I didn't know. I didn't mean to cause any trouble. Not really. I was mad at you for not wanting to look for Dad anymore. I mean . . . it isn't fair. Besides, if the government *is* hiding something that has to do with Dad, I have a right to know."

"Do ye now? And just how far do you think your rights go?" J.B. shoved his hands into the pockets of his black jacket. "I wish you would've talked with us first.

When we asked you to forget about finding him, we knew you'd be disappointed, but this. . . . I never thought you'd go against orders, lass."

"Don't be so hard on her, luv." Gram shifted to the edge of Jennie's chair and slipped a reassuring arm around Jennie's shoulders. "When you get down to it, this whole thing is mostly our fault—and the government's. We should have told her the truth."

"Our orders were to tell her as little as possible."

Gram tensed. "Yes, but the government isn't always right."

This was getting bizarre. "What story? What couldn't you tell me? What are you talking about?"

J.B. ran a hand through his silver hair, walked to the window and stared at something outside. His action reminded Jennie of when she'd first met him. In his rich Irish brogue he had told her he had once worked with her father. When Jennie asked him if Dad was still alive, he'd said, "I don't know, lass."

At the time, his hesitation had given Jennie hope. Now she had the feeling he and Gram intended to close the door to that and any other hope she had of finding Dad. J.B. turned back to face her. "When Helen told me ye wanted to spend the summer hunting for Jason, I agreed. Felt it was about time to clear things up once and for all."

"Here we are." Mom bustled in with a tray and handed Gram and J.B. their coffee, took her own, and sat in the rocker opposite Jennie. She gave Jennie a strange look—a cross between disgust and disbelief—and turned to Gram. "I'm sorry about this, Helen. I knew Jennie was having trouble accepting Jason's death, but I had no idea she'd pull a stunt like this."

Gram sipped at her coffee and nodded. "I'm afraid we all misjudged Jennie's resourcefulness. I'd forgotten how much like her father she can be." Gram didn't smile, but the sudden twinkle of appreciation in her eyes when she looked down at Jennie spoke volumes. Even with all that had happened, Gram was still on her side.

"Just how much trouble is she in?" Mom asked.

Jennie's heart lurched. Trouble? Oh, great. Why hadn't she seen it before? No wonder Mom was so upset. Her daughter had interfered with government affairs. *Say your prayers, McGrady. They're sending you to prison.*

Jennie shifted her gaze from one to the other and settled on J.B. since he seemed to be the only one with all the answers. "Would you guys please tell me what's going on? Am I going to be arrested or something?"

J.B. hesitated, then shook his head. "No. But we'll need to get you out of here for a while. The reporters will be swarming all over this place if they discover where ye live. We're doing what we can to settle things and provide the press with acceptable answers. Hopefully, that will be enough."

"We'll be leaving in a couple of days to go on the cruise," Gram added. "By the time we get back, things will have blown over."

Mom cleared her throat. "I still can't believe you would do something like this, Jennie. Despite everyone's assurance to the contrary, you stubbornly insist your father is alive. You've caused us all a great deal of grief over this."

"He *is* alive." Jennie hugged herself and sank deeper into her chair. "I'm not wrong. J.B., tell her. You said you thought he might be alive. Don't you remember? When we first met."

"I'm afraid that was wishful thinking on my part. Your Gram and I kept hoping, but . . ." J.B. shook his head.

"Before Mom came in you said this was partly your fault for not telling me the whole story. Are you trying to say you know for sure that Dad is . . ." *Dead.* Jennie couldn't say the word out loud. It would mean giving up, and she couldn't do that.

"Go ahead and say it, Jennie," Mom pleaded. "It's time. Please, can't you just admit Jason is dead?"

Jennie stared at the wall above Mom. Voices warred in her head. *Give it up, McGrady. Stop acting like a little kid.* "I can't," Jennie finally said. "I think he's still alive and nothing you say can change my mind. I'm glad I did the show. At least I did something." *Dad will see it and come home. Then you'll be sorry you doubted me.* Jennie didn't say the last part out loud. Even to her own mind it sounded like the feeble cries of a stubborn child rather than the intelligent arguments of a sixteen-year-old.

"I think you'd better tell her what we've learned, luv," Gram said to J.B. as she squeezed Jennie's shoulder.

J.B. walked across the carpet and settled back on the sofa near Gram. "It pains me to say it, lass, but perhaps it is best ye know the whole story. Your mother is right. Jason is dead. When Helen asked me for help in reopening the case, I went right to the top. Asked one of me friends in Washington to pull up Jason's file. It wasn't easy to get the information, but he eventually came through. While your Gram and I were in Europe he called with a full report. According to our records, Jason had a passenger with him that day. A fellow agent. When the plane went down, Jason told him to bail out. The lad jumped, thinking Jason would be following." J.B. drew a hand across his face. "He never did, lass. The plane went down in flames with your father still on board."

"B-but the picture."

"That puzzled me until I showed it to the brass and talked to the lass who took it. As ye already know, Debbie admitted to making a mistake. I'm sorry, lass. I truly am."

Gram wrapped loving arms around her. But Jennie found no comfort in them. All she could feel was a growing numbness. Her arguments melted away like a summer snow. She didn't want to hear any more. Dazed and defeated, she pushed away from Gram and walked to the stairs. The stairs she'd run up and down all her life suddenly seemed impossible to climb. Jennie willed one foot to lift, then the next.

Once in her room, she went to her closet and took down the box labeled "Dad's Things." One by one she set them on her bed, letting the memories soak into her heart like tears into her Kleenex.

5

"Jennie!" Mom's voice penetrated the foggy numbness surrounding her. "Honey, I know you're upset, but you've got to eat."

Jennie placed the box of her dad's things on the shelf. Then, taking the picture of him that she kept on her bedside stand, she placed it on the shelf with photos of Mom, Gram and Nick, and the others. It wasn't that she didn't love him anymore. She did. She just didn't want to be reminded of his death every time she went to bed.

There was nothing left to do now but go downstairs and apologize. She'd tell J.B. and Gram that she was ready to do whatever she needed to do to straighten things out with the government and the media.

J.B. set up a news conference for two in the afternoon in the lobby of the Hilton Hotel. He asked Jennie if she wanted to make a statement to assure the public she was satisfied with the government's findings. Satisfied? That was rich. Her father had been killed and was never coming home. How could she be satisfied?

J.B. told Jennie she didn't need to go with him, but she decided she would—not because she was satisfied, but because she owed John Hendricks and the other reporters an apology.

37

At the hotel, a crowd of reporters and photographers hovered around. J.B. introduced himself as the official spokesperson for the FBI in Oregon and went on to make a formal apology. He told the story of Jason McGrady's disappearance, then offered the same information about the agent who'd witnessed the tragedy.

"Because of the highly confidential elements of the mission that McGrady and his passenger were on at the time," J.B. said in closing, "I still can't reveal details of the case. I can only say that, according to the bureau files, Jason McGrady was killed in the plane crash. Both the FBI and the DEA would like to extend their sincerest apologies to the McGrady family for not providing more complete information when it became available. Because of that error in judgment, we've subjected this young lady and her family to a great deal of pain that could otherwise have been avoided."

After concluding his remarks, he introduced Jennie. As she stepped up to the microphone, he squeezed her shoulder. Feeling more robotic than human, Jennie glanced over the crowd and picked a sympathetic-looking face out of the audience, John Hendricks, the man who had interviewed her at KKNG-TV only a few days earlier. Days? It seemed much longer than that. More like years. After apologizing to Hendricks, Jennie gave her side of the story.

"I spoke with the . . . um, with J.B . . . um . . . Mr. Bradley this morning. I didn't mean to cause any trouble. I only wanted to find my dad. I really believed he was alive." Jennie closed her eyes and took a deep breath, determined not to cry. "I went on television to learn the truth about my father. I guess I found it." Jennie thanked them and turned from the clicks, whirs, flashes, and questions. J.B. hooked an arm around her shoulder and led her away from the crowd.

"How do you know for certain he's really dead?" John Hendricks asked as she passed by him and his cameraman. His question startled her. What was he doing? Before giving her a chance to answer, he asked another. "Have you considered the possibility that the government might be lying to you? Let's face it; they lied once—what makes you think they aren't lying now?"

Hendricks's questions brought a flood of others. J.B. drew her away from the overzealous journalists and reporters. Jennie let him escort her through a side door and into a waiting limousine. Once inside, she leaned back in the soft gray leather seat and closed her eyes.

"Pay them no mind, lass." J.B. leaned forward and mumbled something to the driver. "Journalists are a pushy lot. Have to be, I suppose, what with scrambling for the highest ratings."

Jennie tuned the questions out of her mind. She'd already asked them too many times. Besides, she was certain they were not lying to her. Not that she trusted the government, but she did trust Gram. Gram had told her Dad was dead. Gram wouldn't lie.

"It's time to get on with your life, Jennie." Her mother's words flashed across her mind like captions in a foreign film.

J.B. reached over and touched her arm. "I'm sorry you had to go through all that."

"I'm sorry too. I shouldn't have done that segment for *Missing in America* without talking it over with you, Mom, and Gram. I guess I didn't because I knew you'd all say no."

J.B. smiled. "You truly are a lot like your father, lass."

"Yeah." Jennie gazed out the window. She didn't want to think about Dad or anything remotely connected with him.

They arrived at the house a few minutes later. Gram and Mom met them at the door. "You both did very well," Gram told them as she hugged Jennie and J.B. at the same time. "I think the worst is over."

"Let's hope so," J.B. said. "If you don't mind, Susan, I'll be taking Helen on home. We've a great deal to do to get ready for the cruise."

"Of course. Thanks for all your help." Mom sounded stiff. Gram had said the worst was over. For the government, maybe, but then they didn't have to face Mom.

Gram stopped at the door and turned back. "I want both of you to come shopping with me tomorrow. No excuses. We need to spruce up Jennie's wardrobe for the trip."

"My wardrobe?" Jennie frowned. "You mean I'm still going?" She glanced at Mom.

"We'll talk later," Mom promised, dismissing Jennie's question.

When Gram and J.B. had gone, Jennie followed her mother into the kitchen for tea and what Mom had called a "good long talk." Jennie wasn't certain how good it would be, but she had no doubt it would be long. She thought about finding some reason to leave, but decided she may as well get it over with.

"I was proud of the way you handled the press conference." Mom set her coffee on the table and handed Jennie her mint tea. "I'm just sorry you had to do it in the first place."

"Mom, I told everybody I was sorry. Can't we just drop it? I mean, ground me forever, take away my driving privileges, make me eat bread and water for a week, anything, just don't make me sit here and go back over it again. I did a stupid thing, okay?"

Mom looked at her, all sad and teary eyed, as if she had the most difficult kid in the world to raise.

"Don't look at me like that. I'm not that bad," Jennie protested. "Okay, so I make mistakes sometimes, but at least I don't do drugs. I don't drink. I hardly even date. And even if I did . . ."

"Jennie, don't." Mom wrapped both hands around the cup as if to warm them. "The issue here isn't what you don't do. It's what you did."

Jennie chewed on her lip.

"I'm not sure what to do with you. I'm finding it hard to trust you anymore."

That hurt. It really did. Jennie had always tried to do the right thing. "I didn't lie to you, I—"

"No, you just went behind my back and did what you wanted to do. You never gave a thought as to how your actions would affect your family. You even pretended you wanted to spend time with us, when all you really wanted was to keep us from finding out what you'd done. You manipulated and deceived us, and that's as bad as lying. I hope you realize that."

"I only wanted—"

"Your own way? Don't make excuses, Jennie." Mom shook her head, then continued. "I wanted to ground you and not let you go on the cruise, but Gram and J.B. asked me not to. They want you with them for security reasons, whatever that means."

Jennie couldn't think of anything to say. Mom was right. She had betrayed their trust.

"A lot of this is my fault," Mom went on. "I realize

now that I've been pushing you too hard. Gloria keeps telling me to be patient—that it takes some people longer to come to terms with loss than others. She warned me not to cut your grieving process short. Maybe she was right."

Gloria was the counselor she and Mom had been seeing "to help them resolve their grief issues," as Gloria had put it.

"I'm trying to understand your side of this, Jennie, but frankly, I'm having a hard time." Mom paused to take a sip of coffee. "Anyway, I don't want to talk about it anymore. You've apologized and I accept that. And I do plan to take Gloria's advice. I'm backing off so you can deal with your father's death in your own way."

Mom gazed at a spot in the middle of the table for a moment before looking at Jennie. "Just promise me one thing."

"What?"

"You'll stop trying to find him."

"There's not much point in trying now."

"So you're accepting that he's really gone?"

"I . . ." Jennie wanted to argue, but the fight to keep him alive, even in her mind, seeped out of her like water from a leaky bucket. "I guess there's not much left to believe in."

Mom sighed and took another sip of coffee. She glanced at the clock. "It's four-thirty already. Michael should be here any minute." She pushed her coffee aside and rubbed the back of her neck. "Wake Nick up from his nap, will you? He'll be up all night if we let him sleep any longer."

"Sure." Jennie pushed her chair back and carried her cup to the sink. "Mom, I . . . I really am sorry."

Mom made her way to the sink and wrapped her arms around Jennie's waist. Jennie had been a head taller than her mother for a couple of years now, but it still felt strange. Mom's auburn hair tickled Jennie's chin. "I know," Mom said as she released Jennie and turned back to the sink. "I'm sorry, too. Now, I need you to get Nick up and keep him occupied so I can get dinner on."

Nick's room was nestled between her bedroom and Mom's on the second floor of their restored turn-of-the-century Victorian home. At the top of the landing Jennie ignored the doors on either side and entered the one with big bold block letters that read NICHOLAS MCGRADY.

She pushed at the door. When it refused to budge, she put her weight against it and managed to move it enough to squeeze inside. Nick had gotten out of bed to play and had fallen asleep on the floor in front of the door. She scooped him up and settled into the rocker. Nuzzling his cheek she murmured, "Time to wake up, li'l buddy. Rise and shine."

"Don't." Nick turned away from her. "That tickles."

Despite his giggling protests, she gradually teased and tickled him awake. By the time she'd gotten him dressed and downstairs to watch *Sesame Street*, Michael had arrived. From the sympathetic look on his face when he greeted her, Jennie suspected that her mom had already filled him in on all the sordid details. Thankfully, he didn't mention it and neither did Mom.

After dinner, Jennie excused herself, saying she needed to pack for the cruise. After tossing a couple pairs of shorts and tank tops into her suitcase, she gave up and got ready for bed. She didn't feel much like packing. Actually, she didn't feel much like doing anything.

Since it was too early for bed, Jennie decided to write

another letter to her father. For the first time since she began the journal five years before, Jennie couldn't think of anything to write. Actually, that wasn't quite true.

The words forming in Jennie's head were hateful. Anger ripped through her like a shuddering earthquake. *Why did you leave me, Daddy?* a small voice inside cried. *How could you go away like that and never come back?* Mom was right. If he hadn't been working for the government—if he hadn't gone on that last mission—if he'd gone to her birthday party instead—he might still be alive.

She tossed the journal aside and threw the pen across the room. It hit the window and bounced onto the seat. "Why bother?" she muttered. "It doesn't make sense to write to someone who can't write back." Swallowing the lump in her throat and ignoring the gnawing pain that had eaten a hole in her heart, Jennie picked up her latest mystery novel and crawled under the covers. She spent the next two hours trying to solve the murder of a millionaire executive at Mt. Bachelor in Oregon. When she got to the last chapter and discovered that the murderer was the victim's own fianceé, Jennie nodded, feeling smug. She'd guessed right.

Jennie turned off the light, trying hard not to think about the fact that if her father was really dead like everyone said, she had nothing left to live for.

6

Jennie awoke to a ringing telephone. "Hello?" She grabbed at the offending fixture and hugged it to her ear.

"Hi, sleepyhead. Ready to shop 'til you drop?" Lisa's cheerful voice greeted her.

Jennie groaned. "No. Go away and let me sleep."

"Can't. Gram says she's picking us up at ten. It's already nine. Besides, your mom said you went to bed early last night."

"Um . . . Lisa?" Jennie fell back on the bed. "Why don't you guys go shopping without me? I have a headache and don't feel much like—"

"Oh, no you don't. Gram said you might try to back out. But you can't. This is important, Jennie. Gram's getting us evening dresses and all the other special things we need for the cruise."

Jennie didn't feel like going shopping. She didn't feel like going on a cruise for that matter. "I know how important the cruise is to you, Lisa. So why don't you ask one of your other friends? Like Allison. I don't think Gram would mind. And with the mood I'm in right now, I'd just spoil the trip for you if I went."

"No way. Gram said you'd probably say that too. Hey, I know what you must be going through right now. But we're here to help you through it. You're going, Jennie, and that's final. We'll be by at ten to pick you and your mom up."

Jennie didn't argue. Trying to fight the women in her family was like roping the wind. It wouldn't do any good with all of them ganging up on her. Maybe if she ignored them they'd go away.

Jennie closed her eyes and snuggled under the covers. She'd just started to doze off when the door banged open and Nick streaked in. He leaned on her bed, his huge dark blue eyes staring directly into her own. Had this family no mercy?

"Mommy said to come down and eat breakfast," he announced. "And you better hurry. Michael's here and us men's gonna go to the park to play while you girls go shopping."

Nick hadn't moved an inch or blinked the entire time he was talking. He made her want to laugh. She didn't feel like laughing. Jennie closed her eyes and pulled the covers over her head. "Go away," she moaned. "Tell Mom I'm not hungry."

The bed shifted as Nick climbed onto it and straddled her back. "Get up or I'll play like you're my pony. Giddy-yup!" He bounced up and down.

"Ow! Nicky, get off."

"Nope." He bounced even harder. "Not 'til you get up."

Jennie twisted around, caught him under the arms, and pulled him down beside her. She tickled him until they both ended up in a pile of giggles on the floor. "Okay, you win." She twisted out of Nick's grip and got to her feet. "Go on downstairs and tell Mom I surrender."

After showering, Jennie slipped into a pair of jeans

and a cropped purple cotton top, ponytailed her hair, then made her way downstairs. She wasn't hungry, but at Mom's insistence managed to choke down a piece of peanut butter toast and a glass of milk before heading out the door.

As if someone had set her on automatic pilot, Jennie followed the women from store to store, trying on clothes and making all the appropriate sounds a person should make when having a good time. She hoped they wouldn't notice how miserable she really felt.

Sometime around two in the afternoon, Gram announced that their mission had been accomplished. No one said much on the way home. Jennie figured they were all either tired of shopping, or tired of trying to cheer her up—or tired of pretending they were having a good time. Thanks to her, all the grief they'd put to rest had been stirred up again.

Minutes later they turned onto Jennie's street. Mom's startled cry brought everyone to life. "It's the police. Something's happened to Nick."

As soon as Gram stopped the car, Mom jumped out. Jennie followed. The numbness she'd been feeling all day gave way to a burst of raw pain. *Oh, God, no. Please, not Nick.*

Two police cars were parked in the driveway with lights flashing. One of the officers walked toward them. "I'm Sergeant Jim Shultz, ma'am. This your house?"

Jennie and Mom nodded. "I'm Susan McGrady. What's happened? My son . . . Michael . . ." Mom glanced from the open door of the house to Sergeant Shultz.

"There's no one in the house, ma'am. Looks like a break-in. One of your neighbors called. . . ." He glanced down at his notes. "A Mrs. White. Said she noticed a car out here that didn't belong and asked us to check it out. By the time we got here, whoever broke in was gone." He shook his head. "I'm afraid they made quite a mess of things."

"Is anything missing?"

"You'll have to determine that, ma'am." Shultz stepped aside and motioned for them to go inside. Aunt Kate, Lisa, and Gram followed. None of them spoke as they walked from the living room to the kitchen and assessed the damage. The couch and chairs had been overturned. The lamps and Mom's ceramic figurines cluttered the floor. Some broken, some not. The kitchen looked as if it had been through a hurricane. Most of the cupboards hung open, the contents scattered all over the counters and floor. Jennie and Aunt Kate caught Mom as her knees buckled. "Why?" she moaned. "Why would anyone do something like this?" They led Mom to the couch in the living room and lowered her into it.

"Can you tell if anything is missing?" the sergeant asked. Mom shook her head.

Jennie glanced around the room. The television, VCR, and stereo systems were all in their respective places in the big entertainment center against the wall. Those were the things thieves usually took. "It's hard to tell . . ." Jennie began.

Gram approached Shultz and laid a hand on his arm. "Why don't we clean things up a bit. We can let you know later if anything is missing. Did you check the rest of the house?"

He nodded toward the stairs. "Only one other room vandalized like this. Upstairs—first one on the right. We figure the sirens scared him off before he got any farther."

"My room!" Jennie tore up the steps, the others following behind. She stopped in the doorway. Her dresser drawers stood open and empty, their contents littered across the floor. Bile rose in Jennie's throat. She covered her mouth and swallowed it back.

Easy, McGrady. It's only a room. Just be thankful no one was hurt.

No, she wanted to scream. *It isn't just a room. It's my bedroom!* She felt as though someone had ripped open a secret place inside of her.

"Lisa," Gram said finally, "why don't you stay up here and help Jennie. We'll go on downstairs and help Susan with the rest of the house."

"Sure," Lisa answered.

After they left, Lisa rested her hand on Jennie's shoulder. "You okay?"

"I can't believe this," Jennie said, still trying to make some sense of it. She gazed around the room again. "Why did he have to. . . ?" She couldn't finish. The box labeled "Dad's Things" had been dumped and thrown against the window seat. Her souvenirs lay scattered on the closet floor. Jennie dropped to her knees and gathered them up.

"Why would anyone want to do this?" Jennie asked again as she picked up the broken model airplane she and Dad had assembled, and set it back in the box.

"Maybe they were looking for money or something valuable, and when they didn't find anything they decided to trash the place."

"Maybe." Jennie returned the box to its place and found the eight-by-ten portrait of her father on the floor. The photo lay face down, the glass shattered. Rage tore through her like a thunderstorm. "I'll kill him," Jennie muttered. "If I ever get my hands on the pig that did this, I'll . . ."

Lisa laid a hand on Jennie's shoulder. "Oh, Jennie, I'm sorry. It's bad enough to find out your dad's really dead, but now this."

"I know this sounds strange, but it's almost like whoever broke in here was deliberately trying to hurt me. Like he stood in my room and asked himself: 'What can I do to destroy Jennie McGrady?' "

"I can't believe anyone could be that cruel. No one could hate you that much."

"I don't know."

After cleaning up the broken glass and removing the photo from its bent frame, Jennie took it over to the window seat. The photo was still intact except for a wrinkle running down one side and a couple of small glass punctures near the top. She could reframe it.

By the time the girls finished cleaning Jennie's room, the rest of the house looked almost normal. They managed to get everything picked up and straightened by the time Michael and Nick arrived. Mom had been working hard and seemed to have recovered from her initial shock, but when Michael came in, she fell apart again.

After telling Michael about the break-in, and making sure Mom and Jennie were okay, Aunt Kate, Gram, and Lisa left.

"Jennie," Gram reminded as she gave her a final hug, "don't forget to set your alarm. We'll be leaving at five in the morning for the airport. Our flight leaves at six-thirty."

Jennie stared at Gram, wondering how she could act so normal when their entire world had been turned upside down and inside out. Any second now, Jennie was sure she'd wake up and discover that for the last three days she'd been having the world's longest nightmare.

The next morning Jennie woke up in a cold sweat. She'd had the dream again where she met her father on the deserted wharf.

Jennie grabbed a cotton blanket from the end of her bed and threw it over her shoulders. By the time she reached her window seat and opened the blind, her terror had faded to confusion.

"Why doesn't he just leave me alone?" she murmured. Jennie rarely dreamed about her father, especially not like that.

She left the window seat to get her wallet and retrieve the snapshot she'd gotten from Debbie Cole in Florida—the one dated after her father's disappearance. The three-by-five photo had certainly brought its share of trouble. J.B. had taken one look at it and turned white. The more Jennie thought about the photo the more upset she became. Had Debbie really made a mistake on the date?

Did the dream mean her father was alive?

Oh, no you don't, McGrady. You are not going to go through all of that business about Dad being alive again. It's about time you grew up and faced facts. He's dead and he's not coming back. Ever.

Jennie stuffed the photo back in her wallet. She didn't know why she even bothered worrying about it. Mom was right. It was time to get on with her life. Jennie had more important things to do than chase childish fantasies.

For one thing she intended to find out who had ransacked their house—her room. She sank back into the cushions and closed her eyes. Had it been a random burglary? If so, why hadn't they taken anything? Were they looking for something specific? If so, what? It didn't make sense.

Unfortunately, that mystery would have to wait until she and Lisa got home from the cruise.

The cruise. In an hour and a half, Lisa, Gram, and J.B. would be coming by to pick her up. "Okay," Jennie murmured, "you are going to the Caribbean. A dream vacation. And you are going to forget about everything that's happened and have a great time."

Jennie shoved the disturbing thoughts about her father and the break-in out of her mind. Determined to make Lisa's birthday present the best ever, Jennie finished packing.

7

Late the next afternoon Jennie, Lisa, J.B., and Gram stood at the rail of the *Caribbean Dreamer*, a newly commissioned luxury cruise ship, tossing streamers into the warm Miami wind.

"Oh, wow!" Lisa pulled a pink streamer from her fiery curls that seemed to pick up the glow of the sunset. "Isn't this fantastic?"

Jennie smiled and nodded. Despite the depressing time she'd been through in the last few days, she'd begun to share Lisa's excitement. She felt something else too. Jennie had the oddest sensation that she was being watched.

"Jennie, Lisa. Smile." Gram snapped a photo as they turned toward her.

"Hey, that wasn't fair. My eyes were closed. Take another one." Lisa posed against the rail. The wind lifted her hair when she tossed her head back and laughed. "C'mon, Jennie, stand beside me."

Jennie leaned against the railing, crossed her eyes, and stuck out her tongue.

Lisa elbowed her. "You nut."

"Smile," Gram crooned.

Jennie complied, but the smile froze on her face when

53

she noticed Gram wasn't the only one taking pictures. A man, maybe in his late forties, wearing sunglasses, a straw hat, and a blue and white tropical print shirt, had aimed his camera straight at them. She started to tell Gram, then stopped.

Gram would probably tell her she was imagining it. Most likely, the guy was just trying to get a picture of the sunset. Or, he could be one of the ship's photographers. By the time Gram snapped her picture, the man had disappeared in the bon voyage crowd.

Lisa nudged her. "Take a look at those guys down by the pool. Aren't they gorgeous?"

Jennie glanced down to the lower deck where Lisa was pointing. Twin swimming pools separated by twin Jacuzzis glistened like aquamarine gemstones in the late afternoon sun. She scanned the deck chairs surrounding the pool area and finally spotted them. One thing about her cousin, she did have great taste in men.

"I want the blond. You can have the other one."

"Lisa, stop pointing. What if they see us?"

"That's the point, silly. Let's go swimming so we can meet them."

"Um . . . I'll need to change," Jennie said, hoping to delay long enough to make an escape. She wasn't really in the mood to meet guys. She turned to tell her cousin that, but Lisa had already headed down to the lower deck. Jennie shrugged and turned back to the railing. She watched the taller and darker of the two young men walk from his lounge chair to the pool and slip into the turquoise water. His muscles rippled as he lifted his shoulders and rubbed the back of his head. He had a foreign look to him, Jennie decided. Spanish maybe—or Italian.

He ducked under the surface and shot back up, shook

the water from his hair, and climbed out. The water looked so cool and inviting Jennie felt the urge to swim a few laps. Maybe she'd even talk to the guy. Maybe not.

He toweled off and, as if sensing her presence, glanced up in her direction. His dark, penetrating gaze leveled her before she had a chance to breathe.

He broke eye contact, acting as if he hadn't seen her. Maybe he hadn't, yet in those brief few seconds, Jennie felt as though she'd been thoroughly inspected and rejected. "Creep," she muttered and turned away. "Who needs you?"

"Did you say something, dear?" Gram, who'd been talking to some of the other passengers, looked over at her.

"Ah . . . no. I was just . . ."

"Jennie," Lisa called from a deck chair near the guy she'd been watching. "Come on down. Matt and Dominic want to meet you." Lisa must have connected with the blond while Jennie had been making a fool of herself.

Jennie groaned. The last thing she needed was for Lisa to try to pair her up with a guy who obviously disliked her.

"Go ahead, Jennie," Gram insisted. "Enjoy yourself. If you need us, J.B. and I will be walking on the promenade deck below—deck six, I think. Just be sure you girls are ready for dinner by eight. It's informal, but you'll probably want to wear dresses."

Jennie didn't like being trapped into things and felt like throwing a tantrum. She didn't want to enjoy herself, meet guys, *or* wear a dress. *Come on, McGrady. Ease up. This is Lisa's cruise and you were going to make sure she had a good time, remember?* Jennie heaved a resigned sigh, shrugged her shoulders, and headed for the stateroom she shared with Lisa to change into her swimsuit. She took her time, hoping the guys would get bored and leave. No such luck.

When Jennie approached the threesome, Lisa bounced out of her lounge chair. "It's about time you got here. Guys, this is my cousin and dearest friend, Jennie McGrady. Jennie, this is Matt Hansen and Dominic Ramirez. Dominic and Matt go to the University of Miami. Isn't that fantastic?"

"Hi." Jennie set her sports bag on a vacant chair beside Lisa's and shook hands with each of them. Matt greeted her warmly, his blue eyes welcoming and kind.

Dominic's lips parted in a smile that didn't quite reach his intense brown eyes. "Hello, Jennie," he said in a thick accent that left no doubt about his Spanish descent. He held her hand longer than she liked. Challenging her? That was crazy. He didn't even know her.

"I'm ready for a dip," Matt said, unfolding himself from the chair. "Coming?"

Lisa followed him.

"Would you like to swim as well, señorita?" Dominic asked, his warm baritone voice melting over her like sunlight through an afternoon window.

"Ah . . . no. I mean . . ." *Good grief, McGrady, get a grip. What's wrong with you? So the guy's got a great body and a voice so deep you could get lost in it. So what? He's out of your league. He doesn't even like you.* "Um . . . look, Dominic . . ." Jennie lowered herself into the chair beside him. "You don't have to . . . I mean, just because Lisa and Matt are . . ." *Come on, spit it out.* "Look, don't feel like you have to keep me company."

A concerned frown etched Dominic's face. "Why would you say such a thing? How could I not want to be

56

with one as beautiful as you?"

"Earlier, when you looked up there and saw me . . ." Jennie shrugged.

"Ah . . . but you have misunderstood. I have been accused of this before. My mother would often tell me I looked as though I was angry with the world. It is my way, señorita. Please . . . you will forgive me, no?"

"Sure." Jennie smiled, still wondering about his sincerity. Not certain where to go from there, yet wanting to fill the long silence, Jennie asked him about his accent.

"I am from Bogotá, Colombia. I lived there all my life until the death of my father." An angry frown crossed his handsome features, then fled. "Now my home, when I am not at the university, is with my grandfather."

"I'm sorry about your father," Jennie empathized, suddenly able to understand his moodiness. "My father is d—" Even with all the evidence confirming his death, Jennie still couldn't say the word aloud. ". . . gone," she finished.

Dominic stared at her for a moment, then glanced down at his hands. He'd balled them into tight fists. Slowly, deliberately, he released them, then lifted his gaze to meet hers. "The day is too beautiful for talking of death, no?" Dominic rose from his chair. Even though she nearly matched him height for height, Jennie felt small and insignificant. Like a peasant entertaining royalty. "We will swim instead."

Jennie watched him go, then reluctantly followed. If Dominic liked her, he certainly had an odd way of showing it. He seemed pleasant enough, but Jennie detected an almost savage fury trapped inside him. He reminded her of a wounded tiger in a cage waiting for a chance to escape. Regal, she thought. And dangerous. Why she thought that, Jennie had no idea.

Jennie put Dominic and everything else out of her mind for the next few minutes and concentrated on swimming. The cool, salty pool water relaxed her and changed her own dark mood to excitement. She felt almost normal when she climbed out of the pool and toweled off. The guys, promising to meet them later, went off to change for dinner.

"Oh, Jennie," Lisa sighed. "Matt is wonderful. He's sweet and sensitive. There's only one problem." Lisa frowned and stuck her bottom lip out in a pout.

"What?" Jennie slipped into her white terry cover-up and stepped into her sandals.

"He lives in Minnesota. I don't want to live in Minnesota."

"Lisa," Jennie scolded. "You just met him. Besides he's too—"

"Don't say it." Lisa wrapped a towel around her hair and bent at the waist to towel-dry it. "He's not too old for me. He's perfect."

Jennie shook her head. With Lisa flipped out over Matt, she and Dominic would have no choice except to hang out together—or alone. Well, that wasn't quite true. The ship did have an extensive program for young adults. And she had brought a few mysteries. Even if Dominic wasn't interested, she'd survive.

Dressed in light cotton, floral-print dresses, Jennie and Lisa joined Gram and J.B. at their assigned dinner table for six in one of the ship's elegant dining rooms, the *Paradise Cove*. The girls were just about to sit down opposite Gram and J.B. when Matt and Dominic arrived at their table. Matt gave them a conspiratorial wink as he eased between Jennie and Lisa and pulled out Lisa's chair.

"I hope you won't mind, sir, ma'am," he addressed J.B. and Gram, "but we bribed the maître d' to switch us to your table so we could eat with your lovely granddaughters."

J.B. and Gram laughed, complimenting them on their resourcefulness. Matt shook hands with them as he introduced himself and Dominic.

Matt's appearance delighted Lisa, but the intrusion annoyed Jennie. Annoyed her, that is, until Dominic took her hand and lifted it to his lips. "I hope you will forgive our boldness, señorita." He straightened and gazed into her eyes. His black mood seemed to have disappeared, and his dark chocolate eyes shone with glints of mischief and admiration.

He released Jennie's hand and held out her chair. Speechless, Jennie slid into it. The busboy lifted a folded napkin from her plate and placed it on her lap, but she barely noticed. She was too busy looking at the back of her hand and wondering why it was still tingling, and why the simple gesture had turned her brain to mush.

Their dinner conversation consisted mostly of comments and satisfied groans as the three couples ate their seven-course meal.

When they'd finished, Gram clasped her hands. "I've never eaten so well or so much. I think I just gained ten pounds."

"If all the meals are this good, I may have to become a ship's captain." J.B. patted his stomach. "Well, my dear," he added, taking Gram's hand, "what do you say we take a few turns around the deck and give our food a chance to settle? I hear they serve a magnificent midnight buffet."

Jennie moaned. "How can you even think about eating again?"

Dominic grinned. "The food was superb, my friends, but if you want a real taste of the tropics, you must visit my uncle's hacienda in Jamaica. One year ago he hired Philippe, the most renowned chef in all of Europe. When we go to Jamaica, I will take you."

"That sounds wonderful, Dominic," Gram said. "I was hoping I could find something to do an article about on Jamaica. Perhaps I could interview Philippe and your uncle."

At Dominic's puzzled look, Jennie intercepted the conversation. "Gram's a travel writer. That's one of the reasons we're on this cruise. She got complimentary tickets from one of the magazines she writes for."

"I'm doing an article for them on dream vacations. Personally, I think the cruise line donated the tickets, hoping for some free advertising. So far it's working. I love the *Caribbean Dreamer*."

"A writer. Now I am doubly honored to know you. I will ask Tío Manny—my uncle, Manuel Bernardo García—if we cannot all visit during our stay on Jamaica. He will be as delighted to meet you as I am."

J.B. and Gram excused themselves to go for their walk. Jennie, Dominic, Matt, and Lisa spent the evening talking and wandering around the ship. At ten Matt and Dominic suggested they end their evening by taking another swim and relaxing in one of the whirlpools. At eleven-thirty, Dominic excused himself. "I hope you will forgive me, but I am very tired. I will . . . how do you say? . . . turn myself in."

Jennie chuckled. "Close. Actually it's 'turn in.' "

"Turn in, sí," Dominic agreed as he moved closer to her. Jennie's laughter died on her lips. His dark gaze locked with hers. "I must thank you for a lovely evening,

Señorita McGrady. I would like to kiss you, but it is too soon, no?"

"No," Jennie squeaked. "I . . . I mean, yes, it is too soon." Jennie couldn't tell which melted her bones, the hot bubbly water or Dominic Estéban Ramirez. He lifted her hand to his lips, drew her forward, and brushed his lips across her forehead. Dominic hauled himself out of the Jacuzzi.

Jennie took a deep breath and climbed out of the swirling water. "I think I'll turn in too. I'm beat." The wind cooled her hot skin. Wrapping herself in a large white towel, Jennie gathered her things and eased her feet into her sandals. "I think I'll take a sauna before I go to bed, though. Want to join me?"

Lisa glanced at Matt. "We were going to walk on the deck. Matt wants to show me the constellations."

I'll bet. Aloud Jennie said, "Okay," trying not to show her disapproval or disappointment. "Just remember, Gram wants us back in our rooms by midnight."

Lisa cast her a mind-your-own-business look, and Jennie left. Dominic walked with her as far as the stairs, promising to see her at breakfast the next morning. "Buenas noches, Jennie," he whispered, then kissed her cheek.

"Buenas noches," she whispered into the night wind as she watched him walk away. Still thinking about Dominic, Jennie took a step forward and collided with a man coming out of the fitness center.

She yelped and clutched her towel closer.

He muttered an apology and bent to retrieve a book he'd dropped in the collision. His bald head reflected an overhead light. He straightened his glasses and scrambled to his feet. "I'm sorry," he said again.

"It's my fault. I should have been watching where I was going."

"I didn't hurt you, did I?" He stood for a moment gazing down at her, his mouth set in a hard line. The dark-tinted glasses hid his eyes, but Jennie sensed she'd seen him before. He cleared his throat and stepped back.

"No," Jennie insisted. "I'm fine."

He smiled then and reached out his hand. "In that case, it was nice running into you. Perhaps we'll meet again." As he walked away Jennie remembered why he looked so familiar. He'd been the guy on deck earlier. The guy with the camera.

Jennie puzzled over the man as she pulled open the door to the fitness center. She made her way past the door to the men's room and the sauna, and ducked into the women's rest room.

By the time Jennie had showered and entered the sauna, she had dismissed the man as a threat. The warm dry heat and scent of cedar quickly softened her mood. She leaned back against the hot wood, willing the confusion of the last few days to melt from her mind. Gram's marriage to J.B., the television show, Mom's engagement to Michael, Dad's death, the break-in. *Dad's death*.

"You have to let it go, Jennie," Mom would have told her. *Let it go*. It sounded so easy. But how could she? For the last five years, there were times when the hope of finding him was the only thing that kept her going. "What am I going to do, God?" She drew her knees up to her chest, folded her arms, and let her head rest on them.

A memory floated into her mind, then out again. At the memorial service they'd had for him, the minister had assured them that as a believer, Dad had eternal life. "Even if he is dead," a voice seemed to whisper, "his spirit will live forever. Someday, you will see him again, in heaven."

The knowledge consoled her in a way, but not enough. Tears slipped through her closed lids and dried on her cheeks. She'd make it, she really would. Eventually the hurt would be bearable again.

Hot air burned her nose and lungs as she drew in a deep breath. Time for a cool shower. She stepped off the wooden bench and pushed at the door. Stuck. She pushed again. And again. It was locked. Someone had locked the door from the outside.

Panic thundered in her chest. She pounded on the wooden door. "Help! Someone help me!"

Minutes later, Jennie dropped to her knees. Blood ran from the torn flesh on her hands. Screams died on her parched lips. Maybe she'd be seeing Dad sooner than she'd planned.

8

You're not giving up, McGrady. You can't. Mom and Nick would never forgive you. Neither would Lisa or Gram. . . .

One more time. Try it. Just one more time. Jennie obeyed the message of survival hammering in her head. Using the door as a brace, she tried to stand. It swung open. She collapsed halfway out of the sauna and hauled in fresh air to soothe her scorched lungs. After a few moments she crawled the rest of the way out. The door thumped closed behind her.

It had opened so easily Jennie wondered if she'd imagined the whole thing. The raw wood gashes on her hands said otherwise. Someone had locked her in the sauna. But why? The answer came back frighteningly clear. Someone wanted her dead.

No, not dead, she decided. The person had come back. Maybe someone just wanted to scare her. It had certainly worked.

The muted light outside the exercise room cast garish shadows of weight machines, bikes, and stair-steppers across the walls. Jennie rolled over onto her back, wishing the dizziness and nausea would pass. After a few minutes she tried to stand. The room tipped and a fuzzy darkness blurred her vision. She slumped back to the floor.

Still fighting the waves of nausea, Jennie crawled into the shower, turned on the water, and sat with her head between her knees. The cool spray washed the blood from her hands and pulsed enough life into her to get her moving again. Finally able to stand without fainting, Jennie got dressed, then made her way through the fitness center and out onto the deck.

She'd taken only a few steps when the dizziness hit again. As she grabbed the railing to steady herself, Jennie spotted Matt and Lisa only a few yards from where she stood. "Lisa," Jennie heard herself call as her knees buckled.

"Jennie! What's wrong?" Lisa jumped up from the deck chair and ran to her cousin's side. "You look awful! Are you seasick?"

Jennie took another deep breath and closed her eyes. With Lisa and Matt supporting her, she stumbled the few steps to a nearby deck chair and collapsed into it. "Stay with her," Matt ordered. "I'll go for the ship's doctor."

"No." Jennie put a hand out to stop him. "Not the doctor—I need to . . . get Gram. Someone locked me in the sauna."

"Are you serious?" Lisa asked.

Jennie nodded. "Did you see anyone?"

"No," they said in unison. "We just arrived a few minutes ago," Matt finished. "Any idea who might have done it?"

"I hate to even suggest it, but you two and Dominic were the only ones who knew where I was going."

Matt frowned. "You think Dominic did this?"

"That's unreal," Lisa interrupted. "What possible reason could he have to hurt you?"

"I don't know, but who else knew? I suppose someone could have followed me. I bumped into a guy just as I went into the fitness center." Jennie shuddered at the possibility.

"There were other people out on deck, too. Maybe someone overheard us talking." Lisa glanced up at Matt as if she expected him to have an answer.

"Look." Matt hunkered down between the two chairs. "I say we eliminate Dominic as a suspect right now. He's probably asleep. But if it will make you feel better we can go down and check—that is if you think you can make it."

"I can make it." This time when Jennie stood she felt almost normal. Normal enough, at least, to find some answers.

A few minutes later the trio stood outside of the state-room Matt and Dominic shared. Matt slid a plastic card into the slot on the door and turned the handle. "You guys stay out here. I'll talk to him."

Matt stepped into the room and closed the door. A few seconds later he popped back out. "He was asleep. I told him what happened. Give him a minute to get dressed." Matt closed the door, but in the brief time it had been open, Jennie had spotted Dominic lying in a rumpled bed, looking as if he'd been roused out of a sound sleep. A pang of guilt that she'd even suspected him jabbed at her conscience. *Way to go, McGrady. Great way to treat a new friend.*

Embarrassed, Jennie offered an apology. "Oh, Matt, tell him to go back to sleep. I'm sorry I bothered him."

"It is no trouble," Dominic assured her as he stepped into the hallway. Concern etched his bronzed features. "You are okay?"

"I'm fine—at least I will be when I find out who locked me in that sauna and why."

Dominic finished buttoning his shirt. "Now we must call the ship's security officer, no?"

"Yes," Jennie affirmed. Using the boys' phone she called security, then called Gram and J.B.

Ten minutes later, Matt, Lisa, Dominic, Gram, J.B., and the security officer crowded around the small sauna while Jennie explained, again, how she'd been locked in.

"Are you certain the door wouldn't open?" the dark-haired officer asked. He'd introduced himself as Daniel Lee. Under his polite demeanor he sounded annoyed, as though she'd made the whole thing up.

"Positive."

Daniel opened and closed the door several times. "As you can see, Miss McGrady, the door has no lock. Hence, you couldn't have been, as you say, 'locked in.' If you couldn't open the door, someone must have been leaning against it. I suspect your friends here were playing a joke on you."

Lisa's mouth dropped open. "You think. . . ! I'd never do something like that."

Jennie shook her head. "Believe me, it wasn't a friend and it certainly wasn't a joke."

Daniel shrugged his shoulders. Jennie could tell he didn't believe them and was certain he had no intention of spending any more of his precious time trying to solve a nonexistent crime.

"Take a look at this," Gram announced. Jennie turned to find her grandmother on her hands and knees examining the sauna door. They all bent to see where Gram was pointing. "There are several dents here. I could be wrong, but it looks as though something heavy may have been pushed against it. It's deeper in the middle than on the sides—might have been round. The pressure Jennie exerted from the other side could have been enough to dent the soft cedar."

Jennie peered at the dents—a set of four, evenly spaced— two near the door's edge and two toward the middle. She straightened and glanced around the room. Her gaze fell on the large rack of weights against the wall. "Whoever it was could have stacked some of these against the door."

"Very good, Jennie." Gram beamed. "Let's try a couple and see if they fit."

Jennie started to pick up a fifty-pound weight. "No, señorita." Dominic took the weight from her. "Let me help you." At her direction, Matt and Dominic set weights in place. Four of them—two high, sitting side by side—fit the dents exactly.

"Okay, we know how it was done," Jennie mused. "And I think I have a suspect." She went on to tell them about the man who had been watching her at the bon voyage party and who had bumped into her just before she went into the sauna.

"I know who you mean," J.B. offered. "But I doubt he's your man, lass. Talked to him earlier." He frowned and rubbed his chin. "I saw some boys tearing around the promenade deck just before your grandmother and I went to the buffet. Wouldn't surprise me if they didn't see you go into the sauna and think they'd have themselves a bit o' fun."

The security officer promised to check out the leads and suggested they all get some rest. They took the stairs down to deck eight, where Matt and Dominic said goodnight and headed down the corridor to their room.

Gram and J.B. went beyond their door to the one next to it, which Jennie and Lisa shared. "Are you sure you'll be all right?" Gram reached up to tuck some errant hairs behind Jennie's ear.

"Thanks, Gram. I'll be fine."

"I hate to leave you alone after what's happened."

"I'm not sure I want us to be alone," Lisa admitted as she pushed her plastic key into the lock and opened the door.

Gram clucked as she peered into the room. "You girls really ought to try to keep your cabin a bit neater."

"What. . . ?" Jennie gasped as she stepped inside. The room looked as if it had been the victim of a hurricane. "Someone's been in here!"

"Don't touch anything," J.B. ordered. "I'll call security from our cabin." He put his arms around Jennie and Lisa and ushered them out. "Let's all go next door."

J.B. hesitated before opening the door as though he expected their room to have been hit as well. With a sigh of relief, he opened the door fully and ushered Gram and the girls in.

"This is really bizarre," Lisa said as she plopped down on the sofa. "First your house, now our room on the ship. Maybe you have something someone wants."

Seeing the room had brought the same thoughts scampering into Jennie's mind. "Gram?" she asked. "Do you think they're related?"

Gram frowned. "It's hard to say. I can't imagine what you'd have that would cause someone to follow us on a cruise."

J.B. hung up the phone. "I sincerely doubt the two are connected, lassies. The security officer offered a rather interesting theory. He'll be right down, by the way."

"Let me guess," Jennie said sarcastically. "He thinks we messed up the room ourselves and just forgot we did it."

J.B. smiled. "On the contrary. He thinks perhaps we have a jewel thief on board. It's possible the thief wanted to make certain you were both out of the way before breaking in. While Lisa was with Matt, he may have shut you in the sauna, taken your key, and broken into your room in search of valuables, then come back and let you out."

"Valuables?" Jennie practically choked on the word. "We're kids. What do we have that's valuable?"

"Mom's brooch." Lisa stood, panic edging her voice. "And the ring. Oh, Gram, the heirloom jewelry you gave her. I was going to put them in the safe after dinner but . . ." Lisa dropped back onto the bed. "I forgot."

"Perhaps they weren't taken," Gram soothed. "I would think an experienced jewel thief would know real gemstones from the fakes in those pieces."

"Fakes? I thought they were real," Lisa said, sounding both relieved and disappointed all at once.

"Oh no, dear. The real pieces are in my bank in a safety deposit box with the rest of the collection. I liked the brooch and ring so much I had duplicates made up so I could wear them whenever I wanted. One doesn't generally wear jewelry worth a quarter of a million dollars—at least not without a bodyguard."

———

An hour later, Jennie dropped exhausted onto the bed in her and Lisa's new stateroom. Theirs had been closed off so Daniel Lee could examine it more closely in the morning.

The heirloom ring and brooch, even though they were worth only a thousand dollars rather than two hundred fifty thousand, had been in the drawer where Lisa had left them and were now safely tucked away in the ship's safe. Even though nothing had been stolen, Daniel still insisted the motive was burglary. "They may have seen the jewels earlier and wanted to get a better look," he'd said. "Probably thought these were real at first."

Jennie didn't buy it, and she doubted Gram and J.B. did either. No thief would choose two teenage girls as their mark, even if one of them had been wearing expensive-looking jewelry.

She rolled onto her back and stared into the dark space above her bed. Lisa's even breathing told Jennie her cousin was asleep. *You should have told them, McGrady. Why didn't you? The minute you opened your wallet and discovered it was missing you should have told them.*

But she couldn't. Not until she'd had a chance to consider what it meant. Even now the thought both chilled and excited her. The burglar at her home in Portland, and again on the ship, might have been the same person after one thing—the picture Debbie Cole had sent of Dad.

Over and over again Jennie asked herself why. Why would anyone want a photo of her father? The only ones who knew about the photo were Gram and J.B.—and Ryan. But Ryan was still in Alaska—the one place in the world that was probably cooler than their relationship.

If Gram and J.B. were right, if Debbie had made a mistake on the date and it really weren't proof that he's still alive, why would anyone want to steal it? If it was stolen, someone had gone through a lot of trouble to get it. First they broke into her house and totally destroyed her room, then followed her to Florida and booked a cruise. It didn't make sense. If Dad was dead like everyone said, why steal his picture?

The voice of hope that Jennie thought had been silenced forever punched its way back into her brain. *Because Dad is still alive.*

9

By morning, Jennie had passed off the notion about her father still being alive. Wishful thinking, she decided as she bit into her toasted bagel and cream cheese. It made much more sense that the break-in at home and the one last night were not related. Daniel, after all, was the head of ship security. He saw crimes like that all the time. Besides, if Dad were alive, it would mean J.B. and Gram had lied to her. Jennie couldn't believe that—especially not of Gram. The most likely reason for the missing photo was that she had lost it, or left it at home.

"I'm still in shock," Lisa was saying when Jennie tuned back into the breakfast discussion. Lisa had been telling Dominic and Matt about the attempted burglary.

"What puzzles me," J.B. added, "is that they went through all the trouble of breaking in but didn't take the jewelry. I would think they'd act as quickly as possible. If I were a thief, I certainly wouldn't stop and examine the jewels for authenticity—I'd do that later."

"You're talking about those thieves as though they were intelligent," Gram said. "I don't think they were very smart. Picking a couple of teenage girls as their targets proves that."

Dominic cleared his throat. "Is it not possible the

thieves were doing, how do you say, a running trial? Perhaps they only used Jennie and Lisa as sitting ducks."

Running trial? Sitting ducks? Jennie grinned as his meaning sank through the language barrier. "Oh, you mean pigeons. They were doing a trial run and we were their pigeons."

"Sí. Is that not possible?"

"It's very possible." J.B. set his coffee cup on the table and pushed his chair back. "I do think, however, that we should discard this unpleasant conversation. A private island in the Caribbean sunshine awaits us, and I, for one, intend to take full advantage of it."

"Well said, darling." Gram sent J.B. an adoring look that left no doubt about her feelings for him. In a way, that pleased Jennie. Gram deserved to have a man like J.B. *So does Mom.* The thought came from out of nowhere and Jennie tried to banish it. Mom's situation was entirely different. Dad was still . . . *No, he isn't, McGrady. He's dead. And it's time to give Mom your blessings and let it go. He's not coming home.*

Jennie didn't like the turn her thoughts had taken. She pushed them from her mind and focused instead on the party of six seated in the ship's elegant dining room.

As if she'd read Jennie's thoughts, Gram squeezed her hand. "We brought you girls along so you could enjoy yourselves. With all that's been going on, it won't be easy, but I suggest we try to forget about what happened last night and concentrate on having a good time today."

"Great idea, Mrs. Bradley," Matt said after he finished his orange juice. "From what Dominic has told me about the island, I can almost guarantee we'll have a great time. At least we will if you'll let us accompany your granddaughters."

Gram laughed and glanced from Lisa to Jennie. "That's up to my girls. Are you two willing to let these gentlemen escort you?"

Lisa nodded enthusiastically. Jennie was tempted to say no, just to be contrary. She still didn't feel much like socializing, but being with Matt and Dominic did sound like fun.

"Sure," she finally said, hoping the delay in her response hadn't hurt Dominic's feelings. She glanced at him, but he was talking to Gram and hadn't seemed to notice.

"You've been here before, Dominic?" Gram asked.

"Sí. Many times, Señora Bradley." Dominic, who'd been sitting across from Jennie, stood, rounded the table, and pulled out Jennie's chair. "It is a stop I make when I sail from my grandfather's home near Cozumel to Miami. Sometimes I anchor on the far side of the island. The reef provides excellent opportunities for diving."

"Sounds wonderful," Gram said as they left the table and headed back to their staterooms to collect their beach gear.

Sounds expensive—very expensive for a college student. Jennie didn't express her thoughts aloud, but they did present some interesting possibilities.

They were all to meet on deck four, where they would disembark the ship and take a shuttle from ship to shore. Jennie had just enough time alone with Lisa to discuss her latest theory about the break-in of the night before.

"I've been thinking," Jennie said as she tossed a book into her beach bag.

"Uh-oh. That sounds dangerous," Lisa chuckled. "You're not planning to get us into trouble again are you?"

"No. It's nothing like that. I can't help wondering about Matt and Dominic. I mean . . . what do we really know about them?"

Lisa stopped folding her towel and held it to her chest. "What are you getting at?" Her eyebrows shot up. Green eyes flashed with understanding and annoyance. "Tell me you don't suspect them."

"Gram says—"

"I know, I know. Everyone is a suspect." Lisa stuffed a beach towel in her bag, picked up her glittery emerald baseball cap, and plopped it on her head. "But Matt and Dominic did not lock you in the sauna and break into our room. Matt was with me when it happened and Dominic was sleeping."

"Dominic could have been faking. They could be burglars working as a team. Matt could have been keeping you busy while Dominic stacked the weights against the sauna door, took my key, trashed our room looking for valuables, returned my key, and put the weights back."

"Jennie McGrady, I think the sauna fried your brain. I don't believe for a minute that Matt or Dominic had anything to do with this. For one thing they don't have a motive. And nothing was taken."

"Money is always a good motive. They might have thought we were rich. You heard Dominic this morning. That's what got me to thinking they might be running a scam. He's been to the island before. He sails from Cozumel to Miami. He's taking a cruise. In case you hadn't noticed, all that takes cash—a lot of it. Question: Where do two college guys get that kind of money? Answer: They steal from the rich and famous. I saw this movie on television once about modern-day pirates of the Caribbean. They preyed on wealthy people who cruised from island to island on their luxury yachts."

Lisa grinned and shook her head. "Cool your jets, cuz. This time you're way off base. In case *you* hadn't noticed, we are not rich or famous."

"Yes, but remember what Dominic said this morning about us being ducks—pigeons."

Lisa giggled. "He's so cute when he misspeaks like that. I love a man with an accent."

"I thought you loved blonds like Matt." Jennie hung her camera from her neck, checked her hair, and set a floppy straw hat on her head, turning it so the upturned brim and flower faced forward. "Anyway, don't change the subject. Maybe we were a trial run for them."

"Like I said, we're not rich and famous, but Dominic is. He doesn't have to steal to support his life-style. Matt told me that Dominic is worth billions."

"Billions? I don't believe it."

"Why would Matt lie? Dominic's father owned several gold mines and was one of the biggest producers of emeralds in the world. Dominic inherited all that when his dad died. And, his grandfather owns one of the biggest spreads in Colombia—grows coffee, I think. The grandfather also owns his own island and several yachts. And his uncle—remember the one he talked about last night—owns a multimillion-dollar resort on Jamaica."

Lisa picked up her bag and slipped her arm through the strap, securing it on her shoulder. "Come on, Jennie. I'm as upset about the break-in as you are, but don't let it spoil our day. And don't you dare let Matt and Dominic think you suspect them."

Jennie was tempted to tell Lisa about the picture, but didn't. Blaming Dominic and Matt for that made even less sense than suspecting them of being burglars. "You're right, and for once, I'm going to take your advice. Today's gorgeous and so are the guys. Let's go have some fun."

Lisa put a hand on Jennie's forehead. "Nope, no fever. You're not delirious. I must have heard you wrong. Did you really say you were going to take my advice?" Lisa laughed. "I can't believe it. Wait 'til I tell Gram. She'll think we've died and gone to heaven."

Jennie stifled a chuckle. "Lisa?"

"What?"

"Shut up before I change my mind."

Less than an hour later they stepped onto a perfectly manicured beach lined with hundreds of beach umbrellas and chairs. The crescent-shaped beach stretched for nearly half a mile, ending near a wooden dock. Creamy white sand sloped up from the turquoise water for several yards and stopped at a rock wall. Beyond it was a park, complete with tropical plants, swaying palms, rustic buildings, a couple of volleyball nets, and a colorful bazaar, which Dominic told them was run by natives from neighboring islands. An island paradise—theirs for the day. Unfortunately, they did have to share it with the rest of the ship's twelve hundred passengers.

After helping them stake out three umbrellas and six chairs, Dominic suggested they rent snorkeling equipment, get into their swimsuits, and hike to the other side of the island.

Gram and J.B. elected to stay on the beach while the others changed and set off to explore the island. They'd only gone a few steps when the foursome became two couples. Dominic and Jennie took the lead while Matt and Lisa trailed a dozen or so yards behind. They left the picnic area and walked inland along the wide dirt path bordered by a dense undergrowth of tropical plants.

"It's getting hot," Jennie said as she adjusted her straw hat and wiped the sweat from around the brim and off the bridge of her nose.

"It is best to walk early in the morning. But soon we will swim." Dominic squeezed her hand, urging her forward. A few minutes later, the trail broke out of the jungle and opened onto a rocky shoreline.

"You were right. The Caribbean is fantastic." Jennie drew in a deep breath of warm fragrant air and sighed. "Mmmm. I wouldn't mind living here."

"It is a wonderful place. However, you will soon discover that paradise is far from perfect. In summer the heat can be unbearable, and the hurricanes . . ." He shook his head. "Paradise has not dealt kindly with my family."

The hard edge of his anger and grief emerged as it had the day before. It unsettled her, yet, at the same time, drew her to him. She wished she could somehow ease his pain. "Yesterday you mentioned losing your father. Was he killed in a hurricane?"

"Hurricane?" Dominic swore. His grip on her hand tightened. "My mother, my grandmother, and my little sister died in a hurricane when I was six years old. It was a tragedy, but . . . one learns to survive." He stopped and tipped his head back, as if it had suddenly become an effort for him to speak. "No, Jennie, a hurricane did not take my father's life," Dominic said through clenched teeth. "My father was murdered."

10

Murdered. The word penetrated Jennie's heart like a bullet. When his grip on her hand didn't lessen, she tried to pull away. "Dominic, you're hurting me."

He looked stunned, glancing from their hands back to her face. His grip loosened, slowly, as if he had to concentrate to make it happen. Jennie shuddered. His intensity both saddened and frightened her.

"Forgive me." He lifted her hand to his lips. "I have upset you. I . . . I am sorry."

Dominic slipped an arm around her shoulder and pulled her close. Maybe it was the feel of his lips brushing across the back of her hand, or his wonderful Spanish accent, or the sad puppy-dog look in his eyes, or the fact that he'd lost his father too, but Jennie's heart melted.

"Dominic . . . I . . . ." she stammered. "I don't know if I can do much, but maybe Gram and J.B. and I could help you find out who killed your dad. It might help to know. . . ."

Dominic stiffened. "You have already done a great deal to help me, Jennie—more than you can know. But no, I do not need help in discovering who murdered my father. This I already know. What I need is to find the killer and bring him to justice."

"What about the police? If you know who killed him, why haven't the police arrested him?"

"The policía? Ha, that is a joke. He is one of them. No, Jennie. I, Dominic Estéban Ramirez, will find this man. And when I do, I will kill him, just as he killed my father."

Jennie pulled out of his embrace. "No, you can't. That would make you a murderer too. You wouldn't be any better than he is."

"Do you think I care? No, my grandfather has lost a son and I have lost a father. We will avenge his death."

Jennie wished Gram were with them. She'd have just the right response to help Dominic—maybe even turn him around.

"Dominic . . ." Jennie reached back into her memory for something that might show him she understood. "When my father first disappeared I wanted to hurt someone too. I didn't have anyone to blame, so I was mad at the whole world."

"I am not angry with the world, only with the man who murdered my father."

"I know . . . I mean, I understand, but . . ."

"Do you? Do you understand what it is like to watch your father be gunned down in the street like a common criminal? To watch the blood drain from his body and run into the sewer . . ."

Jennie swallowed and stared straight ahead at the blurring landscape.

They walked on for a few minutes in silence, each lost in their own grief. Dominic broke the silence with another apology.

"You don't have to apologize," Jennie told him. "If you can't tell me how you feel, I wouldn't be much of a friend, would I?"

Jennie stopped walking and turned to face him. "You're right, Dominic, I don't understand what you've been through—at least not completely, but I'm willing to listen and do anything I can to help."

Dominic slid his forefinger along her jaw, stopping at her chin to tilt it up. "Are you my friend, Jennie Mc-Grady?"

Jennie nodded, trying to concentrate on his question instead of on him. "I would like to be."

"Hey, you guys, break it up," Matt called as he and Lisa rounded the corner. Jennie bounced to earth feeling disoriented and disappointed—as if she'd been suddenly awakened from a romantic dream she didn't want to end.

"No smooching on the trail—at least not until we can do it too." Matt chuckled at his own joke.

Jennie wished she could have come back with a quick retort, but she was certain Dominic had cast a spell on her. If she said anything now it would probably come out sounding like gibberish. Instead, she just smiled and pretended he hadn't affected her in the least.

They waited for Lisa and Matt to catch up, then followed the trail again until it led them to an abandoned lighthouse. The foursome wandered through what had once been a home overlooking the brilliant Caribbean Sea. The house lay in ruins now, the victim of a storm. The lighthouse had fared better but stood deserted and empty.

"Neat place," Lisa said, her gaze traveling over the compound.

"I don't know about you guys," Matt announced, "but after that hike, I'm ready for a swim."

Lisa and Dominic seconded Matt's suggestion to head for the water. Jennie lagged behind. "You go ahead," she said to Dominic when he reached for her hand. "I want to get a closer look at the house." Actually, that wasn't quite true. She really wanted a few minutes alone. Dominic had nearly sent her into emotional overload and Jennie needed time to recover. "I'll be there as soon as I get a couple of pictures."

For a moment she thought Dominic would argue with her, but apparently his desire for a swim outweighed his desire to escort her through a decaying building. Or maybe he needed to put some distance between them as well.

Jennie wandered along the narrow and at times overgrown path to the main house. She looked at the weathered, sagging timbers, broken windows, and overgrown gardens, trying to imagine what it might have been like twenty years before. There would have been a sloping lawn, she decided, reaching from the sea to the house where the family gathered on Sunday afternoons and children played in the sun. Anytime you wanted, you could sit on wooden chairs in the front yard and watch dolphins cavorting in the Caribbean. Next to the house she envisioned a garden filled with flowering shrubs, birds of paradise, and orchids, and in the center there'd be a fountain.

A shuffling sound snapped Jennie to attention. Alarm kicked her adrenaline into motion. Someone was there. *Relax, McGrady. Of course someone is there. The island has just been invaded by twelve hundred people. It's probably one of the tour groups.*

The serene mood had been shattered. Time to join the others. She headed back down the trail. When she reached the main road, Jennie turned for one last photo of the estate. As she focused her camera on the scene she noticed a bespectacled figure in a straw hat, tropical shirt, and khaki shorts standing off to the side of the trail.

Fear blazed through her, setting her nerve endings on fire. She kept the camera against her face, pretending not to notice him. *Maybe he isn't watching you. Maybe the fact that he's facing your direction is just a coincidence.* She shifted the camera slightly, then used the telephoto lens to bring him closer. It was the man who'd been watching her the day before, the same one she'd collided with when she went to the sauna. And now he was coming toward her.

Jennie snapped the picture, then turned away, pretending not to have noticed him. She'd get the picture developed on board the ship and show Gram and J.B.

Jennie passed the lighthouse and quickened her steps. Just a few more feet and she'd reach the main road—people. And safety.

She sensed a presence behind her and started to run. A hand gripped her shoulder.

11

Before she could scream, his hand closed over her mouth. "I'm not going to hurt you, Jennie," he whispered hoarsely. With his free hand he opened the back of her camera, extracted the film, and tossed it to the ground. In the same movement, he pulled her against him, pinning her arms against her sides.

How did he know her name? Had he been following her? She struggled to get free, but he held her firm, his muscles like granite. That surprised her. From his outward appearance she'd expected him to be flabby. The balding head and sloppy clothes didn't match the strength in his arms or the fluid moves she'd just witnessed. And something else. He had a gun. She could feel the holster pressing against her back.

Let me go! Jennie tried to scream. All that escaped was a muffled, "Mmmmph." She tried kicking his shins, but all she hit was air.

"I said I wouldn't hurt you, Jennie. I meant that. I just need to talk to you."

Yeah, right. People who aren't going to hurt you don't grab you from behind—or try to fry you in a sauna. Jennie went limp, hoping to catch him off guard. Maybe he'd loosen his grip and she could escape. It might have

85

worked if it hadn't been for his next words.

"I have a message for you from your father," he said.

Jennie stiffened. Had she heard him right? *This is crazy. Dad's dead. This can't be happening. It's just a trick.*

As if hearing her thoughts he added, "It's true, Jennie. I'm going to let go of you now. But I need your promise that you won't scream or tell anyone I've spoken with you."

"Mmmm-hmm." Jennie nodded in agreement. Maybe she'd comply, maybe not. One thing for certain, she wouldn't make the mistake of turning her back on him again.

He let go of her, then scooped up the film he'd dropped and handed it to her. "Sorry I had to do that. I don't like having my picture taken." The hint of a smile cracked his rigid jaw. Jennie wished she could see his eyes. They told a lot about people. Unfortunately, his sunglasses blocked her view. In sizing him up, Jennie decided he was either a criminal or a cop. Her intuition told her it was the latter. *That's nuts, McGrady. A cop wouldn't have locked you in the sauna.* On the other hand, if he wanted her out of the way while he searched her room, he might have.

"Who are you?" she asked with more confidence than she felt. "And why should I believe you? Gram and J.B. said Dad was dead."

"To them he is."

"I don't understand."

"I'm a friend of your father's." He reached into his shirt pocket, pulled out a wallet, and flipped it open, revealing an official-looking badge. "Agent Brett Roberts, DEA."

"I still don't understand. What—"

"Jennie!" Dominic called from farther down the main trail.

Roberts put a hand out to silence her. "We can't talk here," he whispered. "Meet me at midnight behind the fitness center—alone."

"Jennie?" Dominic called again. She turned toward the sound of his voice.

"I'll be right there," she yelled, then swung back to tell Roberts she had no intention of meeting him or any other stranger on deck alone at midnight—even if he did work for the government.

But the mysterious agent had disappeared. Jennie stared down at the exposed film dangling from her fingers. *"I have a message from your father,"* Roberts had said. Did that mean Dad was alive after all? Hope began to swell in her heart like a rose coming into bloom. *No, McGrady,* the practical side of her objected. *Don't do this to yourself. Don't even think it. Roberts hadn't actually said that Dad was alive. He only said he had a message.*

What was it Roberts had said when she'd mentioned Gram and J.B.? "To them he is." What exactly did that mean?

"There you are. We thought you had deserted us." Dominic's grin slid away when he reached her. "You are troubled, Jennie. Something has happened, no?"

Jennie glanced at the film still clutched in her hand. Should she mention her encounter with Roberts? Maybe Dominic and Matt could go after him. If he had a message from Dad he could give it to her in front of her friends. No. That wasn't the answer. If he really was an agent and really did have a message from her father, Jennie couldn't afford to let anything interfere. "Just upset." She held up the film. "Look at this—a whole roll of film ruined."

"That is too bad." He slipped a comforting arm around her shoulder. "You have more film, no?"

Jennie nodded. "Yeah, it's just that I had some good shots on this one." She shrugged and stuffed it into her camera case, giving Dominic what she hoped was a casual smile. "Oh well, I guess I need to look at the bright side. It only had about ten pictures on it. I can always get more."

"I know the ideal place to take photographs." He led her down the path to an old dock where Lisa lay in the sun and Matt dangled his long tan legs over the side.

Jennie loaded her camera and took a dozen or so shots of Matt, Dominic, and Lisa and had Lisa take a few of her and Dominic. One of those captured Dominic carrying her to the end of the dock and dropping her in the water.

Jennie came up sputtering. She pushed her hair out of her face, then sent a wall of water flying in Dominic's direction. He dove in and Jennie raced away from the dock. They played, swam, and snorkeled for about an hour, then headed back to the picnic area for lunch.

On the walk back, Jennie felt as though someone had recharged her battery. Part of her excitement had to do with her growing feelings for Dominic. She'd never met anyone quite like him. They were alike in some ways— both had lost a father and were nursing wounds that would never heal.

Jennie glanced up at Dominic and smiled. He squeezed her hand. Yes, she definitely liked being with Dominic. But that didn't account for the almost raw energy surging through her that afternoon. She was excited about meeting Roberts again and hearing about Dad.

They joined Gram and J.B. at one of the many picnic

tables for an informal buffet lunch of hamburgers, salads, and fruit; then Matt and Dominic invited the girls to play volleyball.

"No way," Lisa informed them as she dumped her paper plate into a trash can and began walking toward the beach. "I'm ready for some good old-fashioned sunbathing."

"Why don't you guys play for a while and check back with us in about an hour," Jennie suggested. They agreed.

"J.B. and I are going to do a little exploring along the beach," Gram announced. "If you girls plan on lying in the sun, remember to use sunscreen. There's a bottle in my beach bag."

Jennie watched them go, suddenly feeling sad.

"You feel it too, don't you, Jennie?" Lisa asked when they began walking again.

"Feel what?"

"Like we're losing Gram." Lisa lifted her long hair off her neck and held it in a ponytail.

Jennie shrugged. "Maybe that's because we *are* losing her. She won't be visiting us as much."

"Or taking us with her on trips."

"Or letting us stay with her because she's lonely."

The cousins looked at each other. "Listen to us." Lisa dropped her hair and adjusted her shoulder bag. "We should be happy for her and here we are complaining. Maybe we shouldn't worry about it. Gram won't just stop being Gram because she's married. I mean . . . she and J.B. did ask us to come on this trip."

"You're right," Jennie agreed. "Gram will always be Gram. And I think J.B. is good for her."

"Yeah. Like Mom said, 'The important thing is for Gram to be happy.' "

A few minutes later, lathered in sunscreen and stretched out on towels, Jennie and Lisa closed their eyes and gave themselves up to the task of improving their tans. Lying still proved harder work than playing volleyball, and after a few minutes of sun soaking, Jennie bounced to her feet, raced into the water, and swam for about thirty minutes. Returning to their towels, she accidently on purpose dripped all over Lisa's back.

Lisa shrieked, then settled back onto the towel. "If you're trying to get me to move, it won't work."

"I'm going to do some snorkeling out by those rocks." Jennie pointed to two haystack-shaped mounds that rose out of the turquoise water about halfway between the ship and the beach. "Want to come along?"

"Oh, do go along, Lisa," Gram said as she and J.B. seated themselves in their chairs under an umbrella. "We saw some stingrays out there this morning."

Lisa wrinkled her nose. "Thanks, but if it's all the same to you, I'll stay closer to shore. The little fish I can handle, but I'd just as soon stay away from the big guys. Besides, aren't they dangerous?"

"They're quite friendly, dear. Unless you step on them. With so many tourists feeding them, they've almost become domesticated. In fact, they seem to enjoy being petted and admired. They remind me of the dolphins we swam with at the research center."

"C'mon, Lisa," Jennie urged. "If they're anything like the dolphins, you'll love them."

"Maybe . . ."

Jennie retrieved the snorkeling gear from their bags and handed Lisa a set of fins.

"Okay, you win."

After buying a package of squid for the stingrays at

the dive shack, Jennie and Lisa swam out toward the rocks, playing peekaboo with parrotfish, needlefish, angels, and a variety of other sea life Jennie had learned about during her trip to Florida with Gram. They snorkeled for half an hour before coming across a stingray. The ray wove between them, gliding through the water like a kite in the wind.

After a few minutes of swimming, Jenny retrieved some squid from the bag and held it out, letting go as the ray opened its mouth. Lisa tapped Jennie on the shoulder and signaled her to surface. "I'm going in," she panted. "Matt and Dominic are back. They'll want to see this guy." She shook the water from her mask. "I'll let them know where you are."

"Okay," Jennie said, taking out her mouthpiece. "You coming back out?"

"I don't think so. Much more of this and I'll start growing webs between my fingers."

Chuckling, Jennie took a big gulp of air and dove under the surface, turning her attention back to the stingray and offering it more food. She mimicked its fluid movements, feeling wonderfully graceful, as though she'd been cast in an underwater ballet.

Jennie could have gone on playing with this winged creature for hours, but curiosity was getting the best of her. Matt and Dominic should have been there by now. She surfaced and swam to the side of the rock to rest and see if she could get a better view of the beach, but she didn't spot the guys. Most likely they were out in the middle somewhere with the twenty or so other snorkelers.

"Oh well," she said aloud. "It's their loss."

Jennie resumed her water ballet and swam with the ray until her legs tired. She surfaced to get her breath.

Alarmed at how far from shore she'd gone, Jennie started back. Something whipped by her right leg. The quick movement startled her. *Probably just a fish. Don't be so jumpy.*

She looked around for her playmate and found him just a few feet to her left. Something brushed past her again. *Thud.* A spear pierced the ray's underside. Its frenzied attempt to escape turned the water around them a sickening shade of red. Jennie whipped around, fully intending to disarm the creep who'd shot the gentle animal. Well, maybe not disarm, but she'd certainly turn him in. Spear fishing wasn't legal in this area.

Jennie looked around again. No one. Whoever it was had vanished, probably behind one of the many rock formations poking up through the sea floor. *And you'd better vanish too,* an inner voice warned. *That wounded ray is going to attract sharks.*

12

Jennie's lungs ached; her arms and legs felt like lead. She stopped swimming and paused to look around. Good, no sharks yet—at least none with fins showing. Most of the people had gone back to the ship and only a few dozen remained on the beach. The other snorkelers had gone in. Had someone warned them?

Jennie took a deep breath and leaned her head back. She should have climbed onto the rocks and stayed there until the danger had passed, but no, she had to try and make it to shore so she could warn the others.

She started swimming again, her heart taking up a rhythm that reminded her of the theme song from *Jaws*. The opening scene of the movie played itself out in the theater of her mind. The shark, circling its prey. Any second now she'd feel its cool, slick skin as he brushed against her legs. He'd make two, maybe three passes. Then . . . *Stop it, McGrady. Just stop it.*

The beach still lay about fifty yards ahead. Jennie didn't think she had the strength to swim that far, but maybe she could reach the dock. A short distance to her left the dock stretched about thirty yards into the bay, like a long arm reaching out to help her. Not only was it closer but two familiar figures motioned for her to come in. The third was already swimming toward her.

When Jennie and Dominic reached the dock, Matt lifted her out and reached down to assist Dominic. "We noticed you were having some trouble out there," Matt said. "Thought you might need some help."

Jennie glanced back to where she'd been swimming. "I did, thanks," she panted, pulling off her mask and snorkel.

"Are you all right?" Lisa wrapped a towel around Jennie's shoulders.

"Your leg. It is bleeding." Dominic knelt beside her.

Jennie shifted her gaze from Dominic's concerned expression to her thigh. No wonder it burned. Watered-down blood streamed from an inch-long gash.

"You must have cut it on the rocks." Lisa grimaced. "Does it hurt?"

Jennie dabbed at the cut with a corner of the towel. "Burns mostly. But it wasn't the rocks. Some idiot out there speared a stingray. He missed the first time. That must have been when I got this. I didn't notice. I was so upset about the ray—and the blood in the water." She reached up and shoved a mass of wet hair back from her face.

"Where were you guys, anyway? I thought Lisa was going to send you out to see the ray."

"I found a couple on this side of the dock," Matt said.

"I looked for you near the rocks but did not find you."

"Probably because I'd gone so far out. I'm sorry." Jennie glanced from one to the other. "Did you see any sharks?"

"Not in close," Matt answered. "A few minutes ago, though, I spotted a ruckus out near the ship. That's why I came in. Must have been twenty fins slashing the water out there. I warned the other swimmers."

"I too saw the sharks," Dominic said. "Your ray may have saved your life, Jennie. He headed out to sea instead of inland."

"Thank God for that. If those sharks had come in close, someone might have been killed." Jennie shivered and wrapped the towel tighter. "I don't understand how people can be so cruel."

Lisa frowned and chewed on her lower lip. "I hate to say this, but what if the person with the speargun wasn't after the ray? What if he was after you?"

"Me?"

"I know it sounds crazy, but after the sauna thing, I can't help but wonder."

Jennie shook her head. She hadn't even considered the possibility that the two incidents could be related—until now.

"But that is impossible," Dominic countered angrily, taking hold of Jennie's hand. "Is it not? Who would want to hurt you, querida?"

Jennie glanced back at her wound and pressed the towel against it to stop the bleeding. "I can't think of anyone." Actually, that wasn't quite true. She'd made a number of enemies lately—she just couldn't imagine any of them coming after her with a speargun.

A shuttle approached the shore, signaling its arrival with a long piercing horn.

"Hey, guys." Matt nodded toward the boat. "I think they're trying to tell us something."

Lisa glanced at her watch. "It's three-thirty. That's the last boat back to the ship. We'd better hurry."

Jennie yanked off her fins and ran with the others back to their beach spot to retrieve their gear, dismissing the possibility that the spear had been meant for her. Ridiculous. Or was it? Again, the balding man in dark glasses and colorful shirt invaded her thoughts. *No way. You're way off base. He works for the government—at least he said he did. Come to think of it, the only enemies you've made lately have been with the federal government. You didn't exactly endear yourself to them by doing that television show.*

Could the government want her out of the way? *Don't be ridiculous. The government doesn't go around killing kids—even if we do stupid things to jeopardize their investigations. Do they?*

Jennie dismissed the absurd direction her imagination had taken and thought instead about what Roberts had said. *A message from Dad.* He'd asked to meet her at midnight. If he had wanted her dead, he could have killed her that morning near the lighthouse.

She pushed her head through the neckhole of an oversized fuschia T-shirt and nudged Lisa. "Where are Gram and J.B.?"

"They took the boat before this one." Lisa stuffed her towel in her bag and donned a white cotton cover-up.

For some odd reason the news hit Jennie like a punch in the stomach. Unwanted tears sprang into her eyes and she wiped them away, hoping no one would notice. Gram's absence shouldn't have bothered her so much, but it did. Gram should have been there for her—to reassure her that it was all a coincidence—to put a comforting arm around her shoulder, clean up her wound—and tell her that she wouldn't let anyone hurt her.

Gram has her own life now, Jennie reminded herself. *Anyway, you don't need her help. You're practically an adult. You can take care of yourself.*

The boat deposited them on the *Caribbean Dreamer*,

and after getting her wound sutured and bandaged by the ship's doctor, Jennie opted for a nap. Lisa woke her up at six, and they spent the next two hours showering, fixing their hair, putting on makeup, and getting into their dresses for the first formal dinner on board. Lisa's off-the-shoulder green satin gown came to a "V" in the front. At the "V" she wore a rhinestone and simulated-emerald pin. The freckles on her face and thick head of copper curls reminded Jennie of the pictures she'd seen of Fergie. Only Lisa was prettier. She looked even more like a duchess than the real one.

Actually, Jennie realized she didn't look all that bad herself. She eyed her reflection in the full-length mirror just before heading out the door. Lisa had swept Jennie's hair up on one side and secured it with a rhinestone and pearl barrette. The short-sleeved, simple-cut black sequined gown glittered as she moved, showing off her slender figure and long legs. Her blue eyes looked larger and darker than usual. For once she decided not to listen to the voice inside that was doing its best to make her feel unattractive, too tall, and awkward.

"Dominic is going to flip when he sees you."

Jennie smiled and reached for her matching black evening bag. "Let's go knock 'em dead."

They met the boys in the lobby in front of the dining room and Jennie wasn't sure who knocked who dead. The guys looked gorgeous in black tuxedos and white shirts with bow ties.

"Wow!" Matt's eyes glistened with appreciation. "I feel like I should bow or something."

Dominic did—and then he kissed Jennie's hand. A bubble of nervous laughter worked its way into her throat. She swallowed it back. He straightened and wrapped her in a warm flow of Spanish words she was certain would have embarrassed her if she'd known what they meant. Maybe someday she'd ask him.

"Shall we?" Matt offered Lisa his arm and they walked into the dining room.

They met Gram and J.B. at the table, and had to pose while J.B. took a dozen or so pictures and Gram told them all how wonderful they looked. While they studied their menus, Jennie and Lisa filled them in on the speargun incident.

"Oh, Jennie, I'm so sorry I wasn't there." Gram peered at her over her reading glasses. "Are you sure you're okay?"

"I'm fine." Jennie dismissed Gram's concern with a wave. "You and J.B. don't need to worry about me."

Off and on during the elegant meal she caught Dominic looking at her—not like he admired her exactly—more like he was trying to sort things out. Sometimes he looked sad, other times annoyed. Jennie wondered if maybe he had a girl friend at home and he, too, might be struggling with the bond developing between them.

On the other hand, he could have been feeling guilty. Had he been the person with the speargun? Both he and Matt, and of course Roberts, had the opportunity. But why? Jennie caught Dominic's gaze and felt a twinge of guilt herself for suspecting a friend. *A friend who had risked swimming in shark-infested water to help you get to shore.*

After dinner they all headed for the ship's largest and most elegant lounge to watch the musical *Grease*. At the program's end they drifted to another lounge to listen to music from the fifties and sixties and watch limbo and dance contests. Jennie couldn't concentrate on any of it.

All she could think about was how she was going to break away from them and keep her rendezvous with Roberts.

She needn't have worried. At eleven-thirty, Dominic and Matt excused themselves, saying they were too tired to stay up for the midnight buffet. "Maybe you two better turn in as well," Gram suggested. "A few more minutes and I'm afraid we're going to have to carry Lisa upstairs."

Lisa shifted her glazed look from the musicians to Gram. "What do you mean?" She blinked and stifled a yawn. "I'm not tired." For emphasis she slumped over and dropped her head to the table. "Okay, maybe just a little. But I'd still like to stay up and see what the buffet is like."

Twenty minutes later, they headed for the lobby area, where the chefs had prepared a long table of the most elegantly prepared foods Jennie had ever seen. Meats, seafood, and every kind of fruit and vegetable imaginable. In the center stood a dolphin ice sculpture. The sight brought Lisa fully awake.

Jennie was too nervous to eat, and at five till midnight, she made her excuses and said good-night. The buffet would keep them occupied for at least an hour.

As she climbed the steps from deck five to deck nine, she thought of a dozen reasons why she shouldn't meet Roberts, but none of them were as compelling as the reason she chose to go. She'd been through all the arguments. What if he were a stalker, a murderer, a rapist? He could have made up the stuff about having a message from Dad. He could be planning to kidnap her—or worse.

Or he could be for real. Her intuition told her she could trust him. And that's what Jennie clung to.

"God," she whispered as she made her way down the corridor and up the stairs to the pool deck. "You've always taken care of me before. Please do it now. I know I'm taking a chance, but he said he had a message from Dad. I have to go."

At two minutes before midnight Jennie reached the fitness center, where she'd been trapped in the sauna. That eerie reminder didn't help the gnawing ache in her stomach. Strong winds caused by the ship's speed whipped through her cotton shorts and blouse, impeding her progress as she neared the bow. She passed under the last light and pressed on into the darkness, stopping only when she reached the area directly behind the driving range.

Roberts had chosen the windiest, darkest, and most deserted part of the ship. Why?

Perfect place for spies, she reasoned. *And the perfect place for a murder.* If you wanted to waste someone, all you had to do was toss them over the side of the ship. No one would ever know. Jennie groaned. Where had that macabre thought come from? *You can still leave, Mc-Grady,* her rational self suggested. *Maybe you should.* "I can't," she whispered, setting any objection aside.

Hearing footsteps, she tightened her grip on the railing, took a deep breath, and waited.

13

"I wasn't sure you'd come." Roberts stood only inches from her and rested his arms on the railing. Jennie turned to look at him, barely able to make out his features. He smelled nice and had changed from his tropical touristy look to dinner clothes—a suit—maybe a tux. In the darkness she couldn't be sure. She wondered if he still had his gun. "You shouldn't have, you know. Not alone."

Jennie couldn't decide if he was teasing or patronizing her.

"You told me to come alone."

"And you always do what strangers tell you?"

"Only when they're government agents with a message from my dad."

Roberts gazed into the darkness for what seemed like forever before he spoke again. "I caught the show you did on television," he said, his voice barely audible in the wind. "Very impressive. You've turned into quite a young lady. Your father would be proud."

"You knew my father?"

"Jason McGrady is an old friend."

Present tense. The butterflies in Jennie's stomach soared. *Don't get your hopes up,* she told herself. But Jennie had to ask. She had to know. "You said *is* an old friend.

Are you saying that my father is still alive?"

He didn't answer. Jennie forgot to breathe and steeled herself against what she suspected would be a negative response.

Roberts ran a hand down his face. "That's a difficult question to answer."

"Why? He's either dead or alive. I need to know. For once and for all, I need to know." Her voice cracked. She gripped the railing even tighter. *You are not going to cry, McGrady. You're not.* "Mr. Roberts, these last few years have been like a roller-coaster ride for me. Maybe it's just been wishful thinking, but part of me has never been able to accept Dad's death. His disappearance was like a chapter in a book without an ending. I can't close it until I have the last chapter. After I did the television interview, J.B. and Gram told me Dad had died. The government even had a witness. It wasn't what I wanted, but at least it was an ending."

"Jennie . . ."

"No, let me finish." She took a deep breath to steady herself. "I would have let it end there, but someone locked me in the sauna last night and then ransacked my room. The only thing missing was Dad's picture. I couldn't help but wonder why someone would want it. Part of me wants to believe Dad's still alive, but if that's true, then Gram and J.B. and the government have all lied to me. And if my father *is* alive, that means he has deceived me too." Jennie bit her lip, unable to talk around the lump forming in her throat. Tears slid down her cheeks and dripped onto her evening gown.

Roberts handed her a handkerchief. "Either way you lose."

Jennie nodded and blew her nose. "Can you tell me the truth?"

"That's why I'm here, Jennie." Roberts moved from the railing and suggested they find a place to sit. He then led her to the dimly lighted and deserted pool deck below, where they found a couple of chairs near a patio restaurant closed for the night.

"The truth," he said in a voice that made Jennie wonder if he even knew what it was. "There's a passage in the Bible that says, 'You shall know the truth and the truth shall set you free.' I hope that's true for all of us, Jennie."

Roberts pushed his glasses against his nose. "Before I tell you about your father, I need your word that you will keep everything I say to you confidential."

"But . . ."

"No one. Not even your mother or grandmother. I believe you have a right to know what happened to your father. Actually, since you were so determined to find him, we decided it would be better for you to know than to run the risk of your pulling another stunt like you did the other day. But there are conditions. I think you'll understand when you hear what I have to say."

Jennie reluctantly agreed.

"You were right all along. Your father is alive."

Jennie stared at him, wishing she could see his face more clearly. She wanted to hug him and hit him at the same time. "Where is he?" she finally asked. "Can I talk to him?"

"I'm afraid I'm as close as you're going to get." Roberts leaned back in his chair and glanced around the deck as if he expected some clandestine figure to pop out of the shadows.

"Why?" Jennie asked. "It's not fair."

"Life isn't fair." He leaned forward again. "Five years

ago, your father risked his life on a mission to bring down a well-known corporation posing as a front for a major drug operation in the Orient. His cover was blown during a drug run from Canada into the U.S. He'd infiltrated this bogus company and was hired on as a pilot. Unfortunately, someone in the company had run into him before. Didn't know his name, but recognized him as an agent. The company put out a contract on him. We intercepted, but there was no way he could continue working that case—and he couldn't go home. He either had to disappear or risk putting himself, the other agents, and his family in danger." Roberts paused and gave his head a quick shake as if to dispel an unwanted image. "Have you ever heard of the Witness Protection Program?"

Jennie nodded. "Like where people drop out of sight and are given a new identity? Is that what's happened to Dad?"

"In a way. As a DEA agent he wasn't eligible for that kind of program, but he did opt to change his identity."

"So what happened? How did he get away?"

"We faked his death. Since he was operating under a phony name, we figured they couldn't connect him to his real family as long as he didn't go home. It worked. As far as the drug cartel was concerned, agent Kelly O'Donnell, the name he'd been using at the time, was shot accidently by his own people in a drug raid."

"But they told us Dad was missing. That his plane went down."

"That was because we needed two different scenarios. And it left the door open in case things settled down. Jason hoped that someday he might be able to go home."

"That was five years ago. Why hasn't he?"

"He changed his identity, Jennie, but not his vocation. He's still an agent." Roberts frowned. "Unfortunately, he's made a few more enemies along the way."

"So Dad's still in danger."

"He's changed his identity several times since then, but yes. There's always the possibility someone will recognize him. And now you're in danger as well."

"I don't understand."

"You know that picture you got from Debbie Cole?" Jennie nodded.

"That's what he looked like several years ago. Talk about a fiasco. That picture was supposed to have been destroyed. She must have gotten an extra copy. Anyway, that doesn't matter now. When you showed the picture on television, you blew the cork off the bottle. If the wrong people saw it . . ." Roberts left the sentence dangling, but Jennie felt its impact as surely as if he'd said the words aloud.

Jennie gasped. The realization of what she'd done sank in and hardened in her chest like a clump of cement. "The picture— the television program. I let the whole country know who he was, that he was still alive and that he was my father." She hugged herself to keep from breaking in two. *What have you done? Oh, McGrady, what have you done? You not only endangered Dad's life, but the entire family.* "Mom and Nick . . ."

"They're okay—at least for now. We've got agents watching the house just in case. Since the program doesn't give out addresses, we're hoping no one will be able to locate them, but we have to be ready just in case. Which is one of the reasons you needed to know. Since you appeared on television as his daughter, you may be in danger as well. You'll need to be extra careful. Don't go anywhere alone."

"This isn't all my fault, you know. Maybe if you'd told me the truth earlier it wouldn't have happened. Why couldn't we have heard what really happened five years ago?"

"We didn't want to take the chance. The fewer who know McGrady's alive, the better."

"So you lied. It seems like the government does a lot of that. They've even got Gram lying."

"Your grandmother didn't lie, Jennie, and neither did J.B.— at least not knowingly. All they know is what they were told."

Relief joined all the other crazy emotions jumbling around in her head. Jennie bit her lip. She didn't know whether to be happy or sad or angry. "That's really crazy, you know. You guys even lie to your own people. How does anybody know who to trust? For that matter, how do I know I can trust you?"

Roberts stared at a spot on the table. "You don't. But I hope you will. Unfortunately there is occasionally some deception involved, but sometimes it's necessary in order to protect people. Sometimes it's habit. Your father didn't want to lie about his death. But what choice did he have?"

"He could have told us. He could have taken us along."

"You don't know what it's like. You'd have had to walk away from your home, your family and friends— not just for a few days, weeks, or even months—but maybe forever. You'd never have seen your grandmother, or your aunt Kate or Lisa. . . . You'd always be looking over your shoulder, never knowing if the next person you meet is going to gun you down. Jason couldn't do that to you. He loved you all too much."

"So he decided to leave us without even asking what *we* wanted?"

"He did what he had to do."

Jennie glared at him, wishing she could see him more clearly. Was he telling the truth? It all seemed so strange. For five years she'd been wanting to know what had happened. Now she was talking to a man who claimed to have the answers. Questions flooded her brain. Dad was a hero—giving up everything for his country—for them. Some sacrifice.

"How could anything have been more important than being with Mom, Nick, and me?" Jennie asked. "He's never even seen his own son. Nick was born after he disappeared, you know."

Roberts nodded. "I know."

"Maybe Mom was right all along," Jennie mused, talking more to herself than to Roberts. "Maybe my dad *was* more dedicated to his job than to his wife and children. Maybe he still is." Jennie fought against the fury whirling inside her. It wasn't Roberts's fault that all this happened, Jennie reminded herself. He was just the messenger. Still, she couldn't help asking.

"Why couldn't he have quit working for the government? Why couldn't he have waited for a while and then come back?"

Roberts rubbed his forehead, then folded his arms on the table and leaned toward her. "I don't think a day goes by when Jason doesn't ask himself that same question."

"Does he know about Mom? She filed for a divorce because he hadn't been legally declared dead. She's planning on getting married. Doesn't he care?"

"He knows. And of course he cares. But he wants her to be happy. Now that he's been officially declared dead, she'll be free to marry again. She'll finally get some compensation from the government." Roberts paused as if wondering whether or not to go on. When he did, it was to ask some questions of his own. "Does she love this guy, Michael? What's he like? Jason asked me to check him out. He's clean—officially. But he'll want to know more about him than that."

Jennie bit her lip. With every word he uttered, Roberts seemed to shove the possibility of Dad's return further and further away. "Michael's okay," she said finally. "Nick's crazy about him. But he's not Dad. Why can't Dad just come back? If he's got a new identity, no one will recognize him. Maybe he could arrange to meet Mom and date her."

Roberts shook his head. "I'm sorry, Jennie. I wish I could tell you everything will work out the way you want. It's not that easy."

Jennie took a deep breath. "I guess not. Still, I wish he'd . . . never mind." Her father had made his choices a long time ago. Fighting over it now with Roberts was pointless. And hadn't she been the one to defend Dad all these years? He was one of the good guys—a man who laid his life on the line every day upholding the law. He was a McGrady. Just like Grandpa Ian and Gram. *And like you.*

Roberts stood. "It's getting late."

"Can I talk to you again? There's so much I want to ask you about Dad." Jennie unfolded herself from the chair and reached out to touch his arm.

"I don't know if that would be wise. If the wrong people see us together . . ."

"I can meet you again tomorrow night. Please, Mr. Roberts. You're the only connection I've had with my dad since he disappeared."

"I'll see what I can do." His voice had changed to a

hoarse whisper. "Good-night."

Jennie nearly crumbled as he walked away. She wanted to run after him, make him stay with her until . . . *Until what? Until you run out of questions? Until he fills up the big empty hole Dad left in your heart when he disappeared?*

That empty space seemed bigger now than it ever had. Jennie should have gone back to the cabin, but she didn't want to go to sleep. What she wanted more than anything at that moment was to climb into Mom's lap and cry. Only she couldn't go to anyone—not Gram, or Lisa, or even J.B. This was one problem she'd have to deal with on her own. Well, not entirely on her own. As Gram had often reminded her, "God is always with us."

Jennie dabbed at the tears pooling in her eyes and blew her nose. She still had Roberts's handkerchief. She'd have to give it back. Somehow the thought of talking to him again cheered her.

Needing to distance herself from all that had happened, and feeling too wired to sleep, Jennie changed into running shorts and a T-shirt, then headed to the promenade deck to run a couple of laps. The wound in her leg ached with a growing intensity. She should have told Roberts about that, and about the break-in back at the house.

As she passed the darkened area at the ship's bow, her skin prickled. Someone could be hiding in the shadows, watching and waiting to grab her. She passed safely through the darkness and headed back into the light.

Your imagination is working overtime again, McGrady, she scolded herself. Okay, so she probably shouldn't be out there alone—especially after what Roberts had said. But the exercise was working the tension out of her muscles, and the wind seemed to be blowing away the turmoil of the last few days. Just one more time around, she promised herself, then she'd go in.

As she rounded the stern for the second time, a figure moved out of the shadows and stepped toward her.

14

Jennie's heart thumped like an overachieving bass drum as she hurried past the man. He followed, caught up, then matched her stride for stride.

"Isn't it past your bedtime?" The voice seemed familiar, but Jennie couldn't place it. Probably because her pulse was pounding so loud and furious in her ears it left her partly deaf.

"Who . . ." She glanced over at him as they jogged near one of the glassed-in lobbies. Light reflected off the wire-rimmed glasses of the guy who'd interviewed her on the television show in Portland. "Hendricks." Jennie slowed to a walk. "What are you doing here?"

"Helping you out. And investigating the disappearance of a certain government agent. I smell a big story here, and I intend to get it."

"I don't . . ."

"Come on, Jennie. You don't buy that stuff about your dad being dead any more than I do. I saw the way they manipulated you back in Portland. The government concocted the witness and his story to cover their rear ends. They get real nervous when the press comes in."

Despite her own misgivings about the government, Jennie found herself wanting to defend them. She ran her fingers through her hair and held it away from her face. "You got their official statement. They admitted that they were wrong and apologized. I'm sorry I dragged you into it. So give it up, okay? I'm not looking for my dad anymore."

Hendricks planted himself in front of her, forcing her to stop. "So they got to you too."

Jennie avoided his gaze and walked around him. "I don't know what you mean."

"Was it that agent I saw you with?"

"Wha. . . ?" Panic snaked out of its hiding place and coiled around her throat, nearly choking her. He'd seen her talking to Roberts. How much had he heard? A fierce desire to protect Roberts and her father rose up in her chest. *Easy, McGrady. Don't tell him anything.* Concentrating on keeping the alarm out of her voice, Jennie lifted her gaze to meet his. "What makes you think he was an agent?"

"I can spot a cop a mile away."

Jennie swallowed. "What if I told you he was a good friend? A very good friend. What if I said I was in love with him and had to meet him secretly because my family wouldn't approve?"

Hendricks's gaze didn't flinch. His mouth turned up in a wry grin. "I'd say you were lying through your pretty little teeth. And then I'd wonder why you were trying to protect him."

Jennie looked away. She'd have to take another approach. "Okay, you're right. He is an agent. He used to work with my father. He was just telling me what a good agent Dad was and how he missed him. We were comparing notes."

"At this time of the night? Sure." Hendricks nodded,

looking a little like a cat with his paw on a mouse's tail. "Know what I think?"

What makes you think I care? Jennie felt like saying. But that wasn't true. Jennie cared very much what he thought.

"I think the reason you're not looking for your father anymore is that you've found him."

"What?"

"I think that guy you were just talking to so intently knows where your dad is and was making arrangements for you to meet him."

Jennie released the breath she'd been holding. "I wish. Look, Mr. Hendricks, he was just giving me some information about my father. I'm sorry you made the trip for nothing, but . . ." Jennie shrugged.

"I'm surprised you'd give up so quickly."

"I . . ." Jennie paused to collect her thoughts. She'd have to be careful not to arouse any more suspicion. "Ordinarily I wouldn't, but I seem to have hit a dead end. I've done all I can do."

"Well, I haven't. The government's holding out on us and I plan to keep digging until I find the truth."

A week ago, having Hendricks's help would have thrilled her. Now it was a frightening prospect. If he unraveled too much of the mystery, he might put her father and her family in more danger than she already had. Still, she had to let him think she was on his side. At least then maybe she'd know what he was up to and be able to inform Roberts. "I appreciate that," she said, offering him a half smile. "I really do. Let me know what you find out, okay?"

Hendricks nodded as he held open the door leading from the deck into one of the lobbies. Jennie faked a smile, then walked across the lobby area and up the stairs without looking back. Had he believed her? She was a lousy liar—always had been. Mom had drilled the message of always telling the truth so deeply into her brain that she practically broke out in hives when she lied. *The truth shall set you free.* "Oh, God," she breathed, "this is all so confusing. I didn't want to lie to him, but if Hendricks gets hold of the real story we could all be in danger."

Jennie entered her stateroom, undressed, and slipped into bed. She wished she could talk to Gram—find out what to do about Hendricks and Roberts and this crazy conspiracy she'd gotten herself into. Gram would help her sort through everything. But she didn't have Gram at the moment. All she had was a DEA agent named Roberts. She'd have to try to contact him. Warn him about Hendricks before the journalist upset things even more than she already had.

The next day, a tropical storm turned the ship into a miserable carnival ride, rolling it sharply from side to side and up and down. Nearly everyone on board—except Gram and Dominic, most of the ship's personnel, and a few other souls with iron stomachs—rushed to the purser's desk to get the complimentary seasick pills.

Several times during the morning Jennie tried to get up. She needed to find Roberts. Each time she tried, the ship's rolling brought waves of nausea, sending her either to the bathroom or back to bed. Finally, toward midafternoon, the storm passed. Jennie tossed back another seasick pill and ventured out of the cabin. Lisa groaned and mumbled something about meeting her at the pool later.

Several questions haunted her and only Roberts could answer them. Needing some fresh air, Jennie tried the pool deck first. She lucked out. Not only had the sun come out, but Roberts, wearing a hat, sunglasses, and another wild multicolored shirt with matching pants, was sitting in one of the dozens of lounge chairs bordering the swimming pools. She glanced around. No sign of Hendricks. Still, with so many people around she had to be careful. She spotted Dominic at the opposite end of the deck and made her way toward him, choosing a route that would take her past Roberts.

As Jennie crossed in front of Roberts, she dropped her novel and stooped to pick it up. If anyone was watching, they'd just think she was a clumsy kid—which wasn't too far from how she felt at the moment. On the spot where the book had fallen, Jennie left a small yellow piece of paper on which she'd written, "Tonight. Same time, same place." She hadn't signed her name. If Roberts found it, he'd know. If someone else picked it up, it wouldn't matter.

It wasn't until she'd deposited her beach bag on the chair beside Dominic that he looked up from the book he was reading.

"Jennie, it is good to see you. You are feeling better? Your grandmother told me you were sick."

"Much. I used to think I was a pretty good sailor, but this morning . . ." Jennie shook her head and smiled. "Guess I should have taken my mom's advice and gotten some of those seasick patches."

Dominic set his book down and unfolded himself from the chair. "I would like to swim. You will join me?"

"I'd love to but the doctor told me not to get my leg wet for a couple of days. I'll watch while you swim."

Jennie walked with Dominic to the pool and stretched out on the warm wooden deck, positioning herself so she could see Roberts. She chanced a glance in his direction. He was gone, and so was the note. Good. Mission accomplished.

Jennie rolled over onto her back, sat up, and dangled her feet in the water. Dominic swam several laps, then glided toward her. In one seemingly effortless movement he rose out of the pool to sit beside her.

"I have missed you since yesterday."

"Really?" She probably should have said, "I missed you too," but she didn't. She'd hardly given him a second thought until just a few minutes ago.

Dominic leaned toward her—his lips only inches from hers. He would kiss her unless she moved. His lips brushed hers, tentatively at first, as if waiting for her to respond. She waited for the fluttery feelings to return like they had before at Dominic's nearness, but they didn't come. Jennie backed away. "I don't think this is a good idea."

If her lack of response bothered him, he didn't show it. Dominic chuckled. "You are right—it is better to wait until we are alone."

His pensive mood of the day before seemed to have disappeared. Jennie didn't have the heart to bring it back by telling him she probably wouldn't want to kiss him later on either. Instead, she steered their discussion onto safer ground. "Tell me about the university. What's it like?"

Dominic shrugged. "What can I say? It is big, too many people. Not like the convent in Bogotá where I attended school."

"What are you majoring in?"

Dominic frowned and got to his feet. "Business law."

"You don't seem too excited about it." Jennie took the hand Dominic offered her and let him pull her up.

"It is my grandfather's wish."

"Really?" She followed him back to their lounge chairs.

"Does it surprise you—that I obey my grandfather?" Dominic sounded so defensive Jennie wasn't sure how to answer. So much for a safe topic.

"I know you Americans do what you like," Dominic continued as he reached for a towel and dried his thick dark hair. "It is different for us. We honor the requests of our elders, even . . ." Dominic stopped as though he'd said too much.

"It would be hard to go to school knowing you were being trained for something you didn't want to do," Jennie said.

Dominic hung the towel around his neck and looked at her. He gazed into her eyes so intently, she felt as though he were trying to penetrate her soul.

Jennie cleared her throat and glanced away. He lowered himself into the chair and closed his eyes. His lips parted in a half smile. "Ah, Jennie. You have a way of making me talk about things I would not say to anyone else."

Jennie sat down next to him and sighed. "Maybe I take after Gram. She says she has the kind of face that makes people want to share their life stories with her."

"Yes, but I see more than that. You have an understanding spirit. What the sisters at the convent call 'heart of God.' "

"I wouldn't know about that," Jennie blurted, feeling uncomfortable about Dominic's description of her. "But I do have an inquisitive mind." She slipped her sunglasses on and flattened the back of the lounge chair so she could stretch out on her stomach. After a few minutes of silence, Jennie's curiosity overtook her good sense. She lifted her head. "Dominic?"

"Hmmm?" he murmured without opening his eyes.

"I probably shouldn't ask, and feel free to tell me to mind my own business, but I'm curious. What would you do with your life if you had a choice?"

He sighed. "I would paint portraits and watercolor seascapes and create magnificent bronzes of children and dolphins and mermaids."

With only his voice he brought vivid images into her mind, and Jennie felt a loss perhaps as deep as Dominic's. "An artist," she murmured when he'd finished. "That sounds wonderful. Have you told your grandfather how you feel?"

"Art is impractical." His voice hardened. "It will not prepare me to take over the business for which I'm being groomed."

"Can't you do both?"

"No. There are other matters . . ." Dominic erupted off the chair and headed for the water.

Jennie turned over and watched him, fully expecting to hear a sizzle and see steam rise as he dove into the pool. He swam a couple laps, then returned to his chair.

"Dominic, I'm sorry if I said something to offend you. I seem to be good at that."

"You did not offend me, señorita." He snapped up his towel and book. "I will leave you now." And he did.

———

Jennie was still trying to figure out what she'd done wrong while trying to explain Dominic's absence at dinner. Matt hadn't seen him since he'd come in from the pool that afternoon. "Don't let him get to you, Jennie," Matt said. "He's a little hotheaded, but he's really a nice guy. And he thinks you're great."

"He has a strange way of showing it." Jennie sipped at the chilled strawberry soup. "Yum. This stuff is delicious."

"Remember, he is from another country," Gram added, coming to Dominic's aid. "Their customs and traditions are not always like ours. You may be reading his motives and intentions wrong."

Jennie shrugged, pretending not to care. Cultural differences? Maybe. Or maybe he, too, realized that their relationship was not a match made in heaven or anywhere else. Still, Jennie was concerned for him. His anger and vengeful attitude could get him into big trouble. Jennie hoped with all her heart that he'd change his mind. *God,* she offered a silent plea, *please help Dominic to see that revenge isn't the answer.*

Dominic didn't show up at all that evening, at dinner or during the musical production later on. Jennie excused herself at ten-thirty, saying she wanted to get to bed early. She'd only been in the cabin for a few minutes when Lisa came in.

"What are you doing back? I thought you'd be with Matt."

Lisa shrugged. "You looked like you needed me more—and don't deny it."

"I'm okay, really."

"It's all this business about your dad, isn't it?"

"What?" Jennie's heart slammed against her chest.

What did she know? Had Roberts talked to Lisa?

"You know—about your dad being dead. You're grieving his death and I should be spending more time with you."

"Lisa, I don't expect you to hang around with me. This cruise is your birthday present and I want you to enjoy it."

"I am enjoying it. I just want to spend more of it with you." Lisa plopped down on the bed and reached for the chocolate mint the steward had left on her pillow.

Ordinarily Jennie would have been pleased to have Lisa's company, but not now. In another hour and a half she had to leave and meet Roberts. The last thing she wanted to do at the moment was talk. As much as she wanted to tell Lisa everything, she couldn't. "What about Matt?" Jennie asked, hoping to shift Lisa's focus.

"Matt's busy—said he had to find Dominic. To be honest, I'm glad. I've been spending too much time with him."

"Are you saying he's not the man of your dreams?"

Lisa crinkled up her nose. "I don't know—it's too soon to tell. There's something about him that doesn't seem right."

"Like what?" Jennie popped her own bedtime mint into her mouth.

"Do you know that he hasn't even kissed me? We've gone for romantic walks in the moonlight and talked about everything. We've had a lot of fun together, but he's . . . I don't know. It's like his mind is a million miles away most of the time." Lisa bit off a corner of her candy and sighed. "Maybe it's just me. Maybe I'm expecting too much, but sometimes I get the feeling he's more of a baby-sitter than a date." Changing the subject, she asked,

"You want to go sit in the Jacuzzi for a while?"

"Sounds good, but I can't." She pointed to the bandage on her thigh. "The doctor said I shouldn't soak it. But I'll dangle my feet while you go in."

While Lisa soaked and Jennie dangled, they talked about guys and how difficult they could be at times. "You know what I've decided?" Lisa tipped her head back and looked at the stars. "I don't need a guy in my life."

"That's a pretty radical statement. Does this have anything to do with you and Brad breaking up?"

She turned and rested her arms against the rim so she could face Jennie. "I guess I am bummed about that. I didn't know how much I liked him until I lost him."

Jennie let her fingers trail in the swirling water. "Maybe when we get back you should tell him how you feel. I think he really liked you."

"He did."

"Then why did he break up with you?"

"He didn't like the way I flirted with other guys."

"I can understand how he might feel that way."

"Jennie?"

"What?"

"Do you think guys find me attractive?"

Jennie ruffled Lisa's hair. "You're kidding, right? Lisa, you're gorgeous. Wait a minute . . . let me guess. Brad dumps you and you think Matt doesn't care about you. You've got a bad case of inferiority. Trust me, you don't have anything to worry about. Matt is probably just concerned about Dominic. I am too." Jennie frowned.

"Do you think they'll still want to tour Jamaica with us tomorrow?"

Jennie shrugged. "Who knows? But hey, if they don't, who cares? We don't need them to have a good time, right?" Jennie glanced at her watch and scrambled to her feet. "And speaking of time, we'd better get to bed."

At eleven-thirty Jennie and Lisa returned to their stateroom. While Lisa was in the bathroom, Jennie slipped under the covers, still dressed in her shorts and a cotton T-shirt. And at five minutes to midnight, she sneaked out of the room and headed to the darkest part of the ship.

Roberts was already there. He seemed more agitated than he had been the night before. "Let's go down to the promenade deck. We'll be safer walking around down there."

Roberts took hold of her arm at the elbow and guided her forward. As they walked, she told him about Hendricks and his persistence in pursuing the case. "I tried to talk him out of it, but when he wouldn't back off, I pretended I was on his side. I asked him to keep me posted. I'll let you know . . ."

"No." He stopped under a bank of lifeboats, took her arm, and turned her around to face him. "I don't want you in the middle. This isn't a game, Jennie. We'll take care of him."

"But . . ." A shuffling noise overhead stopped her. *Crack*. A bullet ripped through the darkness and slammed into the deck where she was standing. Jennie dropped to the floor.

15

Roberts fell on top of her. After a few seconds, he rolled away, jumped to his feet, and scanned the area above them where lifeboats hung in tidy rows.

"Stay down," he ordered as he ascended a narrow ladder to a plank that provided access to the boats.

Jennie crawled to the wall and huddled against it, willing her lungs to inhale-exhale. She peered into the lights and shadows above her. Someone had shot at them! Aiming for Roberts or her? *Not hard to figure out, Mc-Grady.* She'd been the target in two incidences so far this trip—that is if the spear really had been meant for her. But why? If someone was trying to kill her they were doing a lousy job. If they were trying to frighten her—mission accomplished. Jennie had never been so scared in her life.

Moments later Roberts descended the ladder and dropped down beside her. "You okay?"

She nodded. "Did you see anyone?"

He shook his head and holstered his gun, then, as if he'd been trained as an emergency medical technician, quickly checked her over for injuries. "But I'll keep looking. I want you to go back to your room."

"No, I want to go with you."

"You can't be serious."

"Look, somebody either wants me dead or they're trying to scare me to death. I'm as safe with you as anywhere."

"What are you talking about? You think that shot was meant for you?"

Jennie told him about her underwater assailant. "The first time whoever it was hit me in the leg. The second hit the ray. I wrote it off as an accident, but now I'm not so sure."

"Why didn't you tell me before?"

"I didn't think about it."

Roberts leaned against the wall. Except for a dim light reflecting off his bald head, his face was in shadows. "Is there anything else I should know? Anything at all that's happened to you since you aired that television show?"

"The night the show aired, I thought someone was following Lisa and me after we'd gone to the movie. The car disappeared. I didn't connect it at the time."

"Go on."

"Then our house was broken into. Whoever it was trashed my room—broke dad's picture, the box of mementos. Read my diary." She shuddered. "It was like whoever it was really wanted to hurt me."

"Or your father?" Roberts's voice was barely audible, but it screamed through Jennie. "I hope I'm wrong about this, but someone may be trying to get to Jason through you."

"The picture of Dad—the one I showed on television. It was the only thing missing after the break-in that first night on board." Jennie reminded him about the sauna and how her and Lisa's stateroom had been broken into. "Do you think they could all be related in some way?"

"It's possible. But what worries me more is that the perp is getting more aggressive."

"You think he'll come after us again?"

"Not if I can help it." Roberts moved away from the wall. "You'd better be getting back to your room."

This time Jennie didn't argue. As she turned to go, he issued another warning not to go anywhere alone.

She almost reminded him that she hadn't been alone tonight, but thought better of it. Roberts had enough to worry about.

"I'll be with Gram, J.B., and Lisa all day tomorrow." She'd almost added Dominic and Matt, then realized that probably wouldn't happen. Dominic had talked about showing them the island, but after yesterday, she wasn't certain he'd ever talk to her again.

Roberts nodded. "You'll be in good hands. Looks like I'll be spending the day going over the passenger list— get the home office to check out this Hendricks character and . . ." He stopped as though he'd said too much, then added, "Maybe we'll have an answer as to who might be behind all this when you get back to the ship tomorrow afternoon."

Jennie took a couple of steps and turned back. "Mr. Roberts?"

"Hmmm?"

"Isn't there any way you could arrange for me to see my dad? I mean, my life is already in danger . . ."

"It wouldn't be wise, Jennie."

"Please?"

"I don't . . ." He hesitated. "I'll see what I can do."

Yes, yes, yes, Jennie cheered to herself as she walked away. Hope. *Dad's alive and you might get to see him.* Roberts didn't accompany her to her room, but Jennie had no doubt that he'd made certain she'd gotten there safely.

She let herself in, put on her pajamas, and crawled into bed. Her body was exhausted, but her brain refused to give in, dwelling instead on what Roberts had said about checking out John Hendricks and some of the other passengers.

Roberts suspected him. She had no clue as to what Hendricks's motive might be, but the possibility intrigued her. Hendricks had known about the show days before it aired. He'd been in Portland and followed her to the Caribbean. Until last night she hadn't seen him on the ship. Why hadn't he contacted her before?

What would he have to gain? She asked herself the question again and again. Was he lying about being an investigative reporter? He'd said he could spot a cop a mile away. Could he be one of Dad's enemies, using the investigative reporter angle as a cover?

It made sense. In a twisted sort of way.

The only other possibility she could come up with was that the shooter hadn't been after her. Maybe the diver had been after the ray all along. The sauna? She and Lisa could have been the victims of a burglary.

Besides, it seemed more likely that the gunshot had been meant for Roberts—not for her. In his business he was bound to have made some enemies. *So have you*, she reminded herself.

Jennie groaned and tried to force the questions and suspicions out of her mind. Unfortunately, one fact refused to be put to rest. It lay raw and exposed in her mind like an open wound. Someone with a gun had tried to kill either her or Roberts, and he seemed to think she was still in terrible danger.

Far too early the next morning, the phone dragged Jennie out of a sound sleep. Since Lisa was in the bathroom, Jennie answered it. "Rise and shine, darlings," Gram crooned. "It's a beautiful day."

Jennie groaned as she pried one eye open to peek at her watch. "What time is it?"

"Seven-thirty. The ship is about to dock at Jamaica. J.B. and I thought we'd watch, take a few pictures—I understand the harbor at Ocho Rios is breathtaking— then we'll have breakfast."

Yawning, Jennie agreed to meet them in the dining room at eight-fifteen. Even after a shower, she felt like a snail plodding along in slow motion. Her body definitely needed more than four hours of sleep. Unfortunately, she wouldn't be getting any of that today. Nighttime didn't look too hopeful either. She had to meet Roberts again.

Dominic and Matt were already at the table talking animatedly with Gram and J.B. when she and Lisa arrived. Dominic rose and offered her a sheepish grin as she approached. He kissed the back of her hand and held out her chair. "I must apologize for my rudeness yesterday, señorita. You will forgive me?"

"Of course," Jennie said, feeling more relieved than she'd expected to. "Besides, it was my fault. I shouldn't have been so nosy."

"It was not your fault. I am too sensitive. But you are right. Although I must obey my grandfather, there is no reason I cannot paint and sculpt as well."

"You're an artist?" Gram sounded pleased and prodded Dominic to tell her about his work. Dominic beamed as he talked about some of his projects. It saddened Jennie all the more that he'd be pressured by his grandfather to go into a field in which he had no interest. Of course, if

127

Mom had her way, Jennie would become a bookkeeper or a teacher. But Jennie planned to go into law enforcement—at least she had a grandparent who'd back her up.

"I'd love to see some of your work, Dominic," Gram was saying as Jennie tuned back into the conversation.

"You will, señora. That is if you will accept my offer to visit my uncle's hacienda. He has most graciously exhibited my work in the lobby of his resort."

By the end of breakfast Dominic had planned their entire day. Lisa and Matt seemed to have reconciled their differences, but Jennie wasn't sure how she felt about the whole affair.

The one thing she did feel certain of was that, although she liked Dominic as a friend, she did not want him as a boyfriend. Dominic Estéban Ramirez was far too complex, too unpredictable, and Jennie had no desire to expend the amount of energy it would take to figure him out. But there was no reason she couldn't just enjoy his company, Jamaica, and the rest of the cruise.

With beach bags, lotion, bathing suits, and hiking boots for climbing the waterfall, they left the *Caribbean Dreamer*. Jennie admired the island's lush vegetation as they walked down the pier and through customs. In the parking lot, they climbed into the silver limousine Dominic had borrowed from his uncle. "I talked with Tío Manny earlier," Dominic explained. "He is sorry he cannot join us this morning, but is very anxious to meet you. He will join us for lunch. In the meantime I am to give you the grand tour."

Matt and Lisa had taken the backseat, Gram and J.B. the middle, and at Dominic's request Jennie sat up front with him. For the next half hour Dominic took them on a hair-raising tour of Ocho Rios. Jennie's thrill of a front-row seat diminished greatly when they left the parking lot.

"Here on Jamaica, we drive according to British custom," Dominic informed them. "In America, as in my home, we drive on the right side of the road. In Jamaica we drive on the left. It is confusing at first." He leaned on the horn when a pink van that looked like a survivor of two world wars cut in front of him.

Jennie winced, braced her hands on the dash, and planted her feet firmly on the floor. She stayed that way until they broke free of the heavy traffic and headed into the suburbs. At the end of a narrow, winding road on top of a steep hill, Dominic pulled into a parking space. "We have arrived safely at our first destination. See? Nothing to worry about. As the Jamaican guides say, 'No problem.' "

"Safely? That depends entirely on one's view," Jennie teased.

"Speaking of view," Gram announced, "this one is fantastic. Girls, stand over there and let me take a picture of you with the ship in the background."

The park overlooked Ocho Rios Harbor. From their vantage point, the ship looked like a toy floating in a huge bathtub of turquoise water. Even Jennie had to admit the view was worth the ride up.

For over an hour they wandered through lush tropical gardens and along a path that offered breathtaking views of a crystal-clear brook cascading over waterfalls, none more beautiful, Dominic insisted, than those he had seen in the mountains of Oregon.

After leaving the park, Dominic drove them through Fern Gully. The narrow two-laned highway ribboned through a dense tropical rain forest, not at all unlike the forest depicted in the movie *Fern Gully*, which Jennie had watched a dozen times with Nick. At nearly every bend of the road, men, women, and children had set up roadside stands, hoping for tourists to stop and buy a trinket.

"It is how they make their living," Dominic explained. "There is no welfare system in Jamaica, and the people do whatever they can—crafts, bartering—to survive."

"Do you think we could stop at one of the stands?" Jennie asked. "I'd like to buy something—maybe one of the dolls like that woman back there was selling."

Dominic glanced back at Gram and J.B. as if seeking their approval. J.B. leaned forward and said, "The cruise director warned against it. Said we should stick to the shops in town."

"Oh, please," Gram, Lisa, and Jennie chorused.

J.B. shrugged. "Looks like we've been outvoted, fellows. With six of us, we shouldn't have any trouble."

Dominic pulled off at the next craft booth and Jennie, Lisa, and Gram shopped while the guys watched. Gram bought a set of carved wooden birds from one of the men. From a child no more than eight, Jennie bought a crudely made doll with a black face and colorful Jamaican costume. "How much?" Jennie asked.

"Eight dolla'," the girl answered, her black eyes bright with the prospect of a sale. Jennie handed the girl a ten and told her to keep the change. With every braid on her head bobbing, the little girl scampered off to show a woman who Jennie supposed was her mother. Lisa bought a carved tropical fish in blues, yellows, and greens from a young boy.

Their shopping done, Jennie, Gram, and Lisa tried to return to their car, but the natives—a dozen more than had been there at first, circled them. In an almost desperate attempt to sell more goods, they dangled other crafts in their faces. At first Jennie felt sorry for them, then grew frightened at their insistence. She felt a tug on her shoulder strap and glanced behind her. A Rastafarian wearing a dirty red and green knit cap glared at her. Jennie tightened the hold on her bag. As the man reached toward her someone grabbed her from behind.

16

"We must go," Dominic said. He tightened his grip on Jennie's arm.

J.B., Dominic, and Matt muscled their way into the tightly woven circle, creating a human wall to give Gram, Lisa, and Jennie an opening to the car. Dominic hopped into the driver's seat, started the engine, and put the car in gear.

"Be careful, don't hit them." Jennie bit her lip as the dark-skinned faces converged on the limo.

"I've never seen anything like this." Gram frowned. "I wanted to help, but . . ."

"They are very poor, Señora Bradley." Dominic let the car roll ahead a couple of feet. Jennie glanced out the side window into the face of a little girl with pleading brown eyes and matted black hair holding a doll like the one she'd just purchased. Jennie looked away, tears filling her eyes.

"Couldn't we do something, Gram?" Lisa asked. "I slipped them some extra money, but . . ."

"Extra money? Let me guess—you all felt sorry for them and gave them more than what they asked for. Am I right?" J.B. shook his head.

Lisa, Gram, and Jennie all nodded.

"It is no wonder they swarm over you like flies." Dominic honked his horn and drove onto the road. The vendors backed away.

"Don't say we didn't warn you." J.B. smiled, taking the edge off his I-told-you-so.

"I'm glad we stopped." Gram punched his arm playfully. "We may not be able to end their poverty, but we've at least given some of them food for a few days."

"You sound like Tío Manny," Dominic said as he speeded up and negotiated a sharp turn. "He has created many more jobs than necessary at his resort. He and his wife, Maria, do much to try to reduce the poverty here."

"Your uncle sounds like a generous man." Gram lifted her wooden birds, admiring them. "I can't wait to meet him."

A few minutes later, Dominic drove the car through the gates of an upscale resort on a hill overlooking the Ocho Rios harbor.

Uncle Manny, whom Dominic introduced as Señor Manuel Bernardo García, his mother's brother, greeted them as they entered the lobby. Dominic's uncle was cute, Jennie decided—nearly as wide as he was tall and as jovial as Dominic was intense.

"I am honored to meet you," he said, bowing slightly.

Jennie couldn't help thinking that if he bowed any more he was likely to roll away. "I trust my nephew treated you well this morning."

"Very well, thank you," Gram said. "I've been looking forward to our visit. Jamaica is most impressive. Did Dominic tell you I was a writer?"

"Sí, señora. And I would be delighted to have you stay as long as you like—as you Americanos say—on the house."

"Thank you for your kind offer, but unfortunately, we'll only be in Ocho Rios for the day."

He seemed genuinely disappointed. "Then you must come back when you can stay longer." He showed them around the vast gardenlike lobby and into a tiled courtyard with a fountain at its center. Señor García seated them at a table in the courtyard off the restaurant and signaled for a waiter.

Within moments their table was laden with iced tea, crisp green salads, fruits, and a wide selection of freshly prepared seafood.

"This looks wonderful," Gram said, "but will it be safe for us to eat the fruits and vegetables? I understand that we need to be careful of the water and uncooked foods as they can cause some rather unpleasant symptoms."

"Ah," Señor García grinned. "That is wise advice. But be assured, the food here is safe." He held up a bunch of red grapes. "Flown in from Florida only this morning." He set the grapes on his plate, then lifted the water goblet as though he were offering a toast. "The resort has its own processing plant. Rest assured, my friends. It is pure as God himself."

That seemed to satisfy Gram and J.B. While they ate, Gram took pages of notes and promised Señor García that she would include his resort in her segment on places to stay in Ocho Rios. Before they left, Dominic showed them three of his watercolor paintings. One was of sailboats with mountains as a backdrop.

"Wow!" Jennie gazed up at the framed canvas. "You really can paint. I'm impressed. Is this a real place?"

"Sí. I am surprised you do not recognize it. This is from a photo that was taken of the sailboats on your Columbia River. That is Hood Mountain in the background."

"Mount Hood!" Jennie studied the painting, amazed at how he'd captured the wind and the sunlight on the water. "How many times have you visited Oregon?"

"Two, three times, maybe."

"Dominic, these are truly exquisite." Gram put on her glasses so she could examine them more closely. "The blend of colors . . ."

Dominic seemed pleased. "This one," he said, pointing to the watercolor he'd done of two children at the seashore, "was from a photograph taken of my sister and me—and my mother."

"Would you ever consider doing a show?" Gram asked. "I have some friends in the States who would love to feature you. And I could do an article . . ."

Dominic's muscles stiffened beneath Jennie's hand. He shook his head. "Thank you, señora, but I cannot."

Gram smiled in understanding. "Of course, but perhaps someday."

"Perhaps."

"You said you sculpt as well. Is this one?" Gram walked over to a large bust that stood on a pedestal.

Dominic nodded. "My grandfather."

A gold plaque beneath the bust read *Juan Carlos Ramirez*. Jennie looked from the older man's face back to Dominic's. "You look like him."

"And my father."

They did look alike, but there were subtle differences. The bust revealed a regal man who could be as hard and unapproachable as the bronze he'd been cast in. His stern expression told Jennie he was a man who knew what he wanted and usually got it. No wonder Dominic didn't feel he could go against his wishes.

At two in the afternoon, they said goodbye to Dominic's uncle and resumed their tour of Jamaica. Dominic drove them to Dunn River Falls, the waterfall they'd heard so much about. They changed into swimsuits at the resort and, after abandoning their clothes and belongings in the car, set out to climb the falls. Milky white water cascaded down a sloping hill that went on for what J.B. guessed to be about a mile. They entered the water and began their climb to the top.

By the time they reached the upper portion of the falls, they were exhilarated, exhausted, soaked, and bruised in half a dozen places from falling on the slippery rocks. Jennie would have repeated the experience if they hadn't had to be back on board ship by four P.M.

With thirty minutes to spare, Dominic pulled up to the dock and dropped everyone off. "I must return the car to Tío Manny. Would you please stay with me, Jennie? I would like your company."

Jennie shrugged. "Sure, if it's okay with Gram."

He glanced through the door at Gram. "Señora Bradley?"

Gram and J.B. looked at each other, then at Jennie. "I don't see why not. Just make sure you don't miss the boat."

Dominic agreed. As he backed the limo around, Jennie twisted in her seat. Gram waved, then disappeared inside the customs office. Jennie's stomach lurched as though she'd just dropped ten floors on a fast elevator. Funny how seeing Gram disappear like that could cause such a strong reaction.

Dominic grinned and took hold of her hand. "Did you have a pleasant day, Jennie?"

"Super."

"Jamaica is one of the loveliest islands in the Caribbean."

They made small talk on the short drive to the resort and during the walk back. When they arrived at the customs office at five till four, Jennie breathed a sigh of relief. "Made it." Jennie smiled back at Dominic as she handed her bag to the inspections officer at the counter.

"Did you have any doubt?" Dominic's smile faded. He stared at something behind her and she turned to follow his gaze. The official behind the counter had dumped the contents on a table and opened the zippered compartment. He pulled out two small plastic bags Jennie had never seen before. Panic oozed into her body like a toxic chemical and spread to every fiber of her being.

It didn't take a genius to figure out what the white powder was or what was about to happen. "That isn't mine," Jennie insisted. "Dominic, tell them it isn't mine."

Dominic didn't answer. He just stood there, his face revealing a blend of concern, anger, and disgust.

"You will come with me, please." The officer took hold of her arm and propelled her forward.

"What's going on? That isn't mine. Please listen to me. I have to get on board the ship."

"You will not be going anywhere," the official said. Two armed guards appeared on either side of her. "You are under arrest for possession of narcotics and drug trafficking."

17

"I can't believe this. I'm innocent." Indignant and angry tears filled Jennie's eyes as she pleaded her case. Her arguments fell on closed ears. Either the guards couldn't speak English or they'd heard it all before.

"This is crazy. It can't be happening." Jennie took a couple of deep breaths to calm her rising fears. Her world was crashing down around her. She had to stay calm. *Get a grip, McGrady. You're not going down without a fight. Think. There has to be a way out of this.* Gram. She had to get hold of Gram.

"Can't you at least call my grandmother? She's on the ship. I need to let her know . . ."

"In due time, miss," the arresting officer said. So they could speak English—and quite well. She supposed they had to with all the American-speaking tourists coming through.

"What about the guy I came in with—Dominic? I want to talk to him."

"Mr. Ramirez is being detained. As soon as we finish questioning him, you may speak with him."

"Then let me call the American Embassy. I have a right to do that, don't I?"

The official who found the cocaine ignored her and

instead nodded his head toward a door at the opposite side of the customs office.

The guards escorted her into a tiny room. After depositing her in a chair next to a battered wooden table, they took their positions near the door and stood at attention. Legs together, rifles cocked and ready to fire if she made a wrong move.

"This is insane. You can't treat me like this. There are laws protecting American citizens."

One of the guards aimed his rifle at her. "Quiet."

Jennie gasped and pressed her back against the chair. He wouldn't shoot her, would he? It would be an international incident. The President . . . *Who are you kidding, McGrady? You got caught with the goods. With the war against drugs, the only ones who would sympathize would be the drug dealers. All you can do now is pray they release Dominic so he can get word to Gram and J.B.*

Jennie tried not to imagine what would happen if they kept her. She'd heard about people being thrown into prisons in other countries, where prisoners were tortured and nearly starved to death. "Oh, God, no. Please help me," she whimpered. "Don't let me go to prison. I didn't do anything wrong."

Jennie spent the next hour praying and trying to think positively. Maybe Gram would miss her and come back to find her. Maybe they'd let Dominic go back to the ship to tell the others. *And maybe you'll spend the rest of your life in a rat-infested prison.*

Jennie squeezed her eyes shut to block the images forming in her mind. She clenched her fists, trying to stay calm, trying not to cry.

"Jennie!"

Dominic was back. She bounced to her feet and threw

her arms around his neck. Her imprisoned tears flowed onto his shirt.

"Hush, querida. Please do not cry." He stroked her hair and held her, but Jennie could feel his discomfort. Did he think the drugs were hers?

"Dominic," she said, pulling away from him to wipe her nose on a tissue she found in her shorts pocket. "I didn't do it. That cocaine isn't mine. You've got to believe me."

Dominic frowned. "I will try to believe you, but why would someone put drugs in your bag?"

"Maybe someone bought them and used me to smuggle them on board the ship."

"It is such a small amount to smuggle on board, and who would be so wicked as to do such a thing?"

"Oh, Dominic, I don't know." Jennie heaved a deep, shuddering sigh. "The only other thing I can think of is that someone wants me off the ship, away from Gram and J.B. and . . ." *Roberts.* She almost said his name out loud but stopped. "Forget it. That idea is even crazier than the first." *No, it isn't, McGrady. After what's happened it makes perfect sense.* Jennie pushed the menacing thoughts away. She couldn't talk to Dominic about it, and right now she had to concentrate on getting out of there and back to the ship.

"What is it, querida? What are you thinking?"

"It isn't important. Look, I don't know why this has happened. All I know is that I'm innocent. Someone planted that stuff in my bag—either when we stopped in Fern Gully, or while we were at Dunn Falls. I've got to get out of here. You haven't been arrested. Maybe they'd let you call Gram."

"It's too late for that, miss." The voice belonged not

to Dominic but to the official who had detained her. "The ship left fifteen minutes ago." He stood in the doorway between the two guards, his arms crossed, looking as though he enjoyed tormenting her.

For a moment, Jennie thought of throwing a punch at him. While he lay on the floor, temporarily immobilized from having his breath knocked out of him, she'd grab the two guards and ram their heads together. Then she and Dominic could run for it. *Right, McGrady.*

Feeling the hope drain out of her, Jennie closed her eyes. Dominic wrapped his arms around her and whispered in her ear. "Do not worry, querida. I will get you out of here."

"Can you do that?"

"Perhaps." His voice dropped even lower. "Tío Manny is well known here. If I tell them I am his nephew and offer them some dinero . . ."

"You mean bribe them?" Jennie squeaked.

"Stay here." Dominic let her go and walked over to the official. She couldn't hear what he said, but the official nodded and the two men left the room, closing the door behind him.

A few minutes later, the official stepped back into the room and dismissed the guards. He leaned toward her, a cigar in his mouth and yellow-stained teeth holding it in place as he talked. A bulge in his shirt pocket left no doubt in Jennie's mind that Dominic had bought her freedom. "It appears that we have made a mistake. You are free to go."

Dominic took her arm the moment she stepped out of the room.

"Where are we going?"

"Tío Manny's."

"Oh, Dominic, I don't know how to thank you. I don't mean to sound ungrateful, but how will I get back to the boat?"

"This is not a problem. I have a plan. We will spend the night here with my uncle."

"But—"

"Do not worry, señorita," Dominic interrupted. "My intentions are honorable. You will have your own room."

"Great, but that wasn't what I was going to say." Jennie smiled. He really was a thoughtful guy. "I was just hoping we could take a motorboat and try to catch them tonight."

"I know you are anxious to catch the ship, but no. It is already getting dark. We will stay here tonight, get a good night's rest. In the morning we will fly to Georgetown on Grand Cayman. We can meet the ship there."

Jennie didn't argue. Having a room of her own in a luxurious resort and getting a good night's sleep sounded infinitely more appealing than trying to catch up to a fast-moving cruise ship in the dark.

Señor García embraced them both and treated her as though she were a gift from heaven. "I want to hear all about your ordeal, Señorita McGrady, but first, as you say, you must call your grandmother. She will be worried."

Jennie placed her call and Gram answered. "Jennie. Thank goodness, we were getting worried. Where are you?"

"At Dominic's uncle's place in Ocho Rios." She told Gram about the customs official and the cocaine.

"That's terrible. I cannot believe no one called to let me know."

"I can. The guy was a total jerk. Dominic bribed him to let me go."

"Well, we can deal with him later. I'm just grateful you're safe and that Dominic was with you." She paused. "You are safe, aren't you? I mean, you'll be okay there?"

"I'm fine. Dominic says we can fly to Grand Cayman tomorrow morning and meet the ship. I'll see you then."

Jennie hung up feeling despondent—as if the only line linking her to safety had been cut. She'd assured Gram that she felt fine. Only she didn't feel fine at all. Despite the elegant surroundings and Dominic and his uncle's kindness, Jennie felt lonely and afraid and vulnerable.

"You must be Jennie." A dark-haired woman in a bright multicolored cotton-gauze dress reached out and grasped Jennie's hands in hers. "I'm Maria. Manny's wife. Dominic told us what happened."

Mrs. García was a beautiful woman, tall—Jennie's height—and obviously a few years younger than her husband.

"I hope he also told you I was innocent," Jennie heard herself saying. "I don't use drugs, Mrs. García."

"Of course you don't. Oh, but you must call me Maria." She smiled, and the acceptance in her nearly black eyes banished Jennie's discomfort.

"Come. I'll show you to your room." Jennie followed Maria up a wide staircase and along a veranda overlooking the courtyard where they'd eaten lunch. Maria opened the second door down and stood aside to let Jennie in.

Jennie's mouth gaped. "Wow. It's gorgeous." The room was equipped with a king-size bed, a whirlpool, and a balcony that overlooked another large courtyard.

"I think you'll be comfortable here. If you need anything just give room service a call. Dominic will come by to escort you to dinner." Maria started to go, then turned. "We will have dinner at eight. That should give you time to freshen up. Manny likes us to dress for dinner—a throwback to the old days when men were in charge." She laughed and touched Jennie's shoulder. "I let him think he still is from time to time."

Jennie wondered if they'd mind her showing up at dinner in her shorts and T-shirt. "I'm afraid I don't have anything to wear except what I've got on."

"That's all been taken care of. Dominic told me your clothes are still on the ship. Since we are close to the same size, I'll go through my closets and find some fresh clothes for you to wear."

"You don't have to do that."

"Nonsense. My treat. It's not everyday I get to play aunt to my favorite nephew and his friends. You just relax and I'll send one of the maids up in a few minutes."

"Relax," Jennie said to her mirror image after Maria had gone. "If only I could." Jennie flopped onto the bed, spread out her arms, and stared at the ceiling. Roberts had told her to be careful. She had been. He'd told her to stay with someone. She'd done that too.

Jennie felt as though she'd been locked in a vault. Every few hours the walls seemed to move in on her. Any time now they might close the gap and crush her. What upset her most was that she couldn't fight back. She had no idea who was out to get her, and no clue as to what the next move might be.

"And that means you'd better keep your eyes open," she told herself. Somewhere below her, water splashed in a concrete fountain. Birds tweeped and the scent of some exotic flower wafted into the room. Her eyelids drifted closed.

A knock at the door jolted her out of her lethargy. So much for keeping her eyes open. Jennie rolled off the bed and opened the door. A wrinkled dark-skinned woman not more than four feet tall handed Jennie the clothes Maria had promised.

Jennie showered and dressed in a white gauzy dress, then braided her hair. While she waited for Dominic to pick her up, she wandered out onto the balcony. Dominic and his uncle stood in the courtyard near a fountain in another of the many gardens.

"It is not right," Manny said.

"What choice do I have? Grandfather will have his way regardless of what we say. It is better if I . . ." As if sensing her presence, Dominic glanced up in her direction. He smiled and waved, then turned back to Manny and began speaking in Spanish.

Jennie faded back into the room, embarrassed that they'd seen her and upset that they'd finished their conversation in a language she couldn't understand.

A few minutes later, Dominic arrived.

"I'm sorry about that," she said, pointing toward the balcony. "I didn't mean to eavesdrop."

Dominic frowned. "It is not your fault. Tío Manny should not have brought up such a delicate subject in so public a place."

When Dominic didn't volunteer any more information Jennie let the issue drop. She'd heard enough to make an educated guess as to what they'd been discussing. Apparently she wasn't the only one who thought Dominic should disregard his grandfather's wishes and study art.

The rest of the evening played like a romance novel. The Garcías were the most gracious people she'd ever met. And Dominic was perfect. So perfect, in fact, that Jennie was almost ready to reconsider the boyfriend thing. After dinner they spent about an hour wandering around the grounds.

"Ah, querida, I hate for the evening to end, I wish . . ." He sighed. "You have had a long and tiring day." Dominic slid an arm around her shoulder and drew her closer.

She basked in the sweet scent of the delicate white flowers surrounding them. Gardenias, she guessed. "That name . . . querida . . . you keep calling me that. What does it mean?"

Dominic smiled and pressed his lips to her hair. "I will tell you if you promise not to be angry with me."

"Why?" Jennie shifted so she could look at him. "Is it something bad?"

He chuckled, the moonlight reflecting in his dark eyes. "No, not bad. It is a term of endearment. In your country you might say dear, or darling. Querida means beloved."

"It's a lovely name." Jennie smiled up at him. "Do you really see me that way, Dominic? Or is it just a name you use to flatter all your girl friends?"

Dominic didn't answer. He was staring into the garden. Had she hurt his feelings? Maybe he really did think of her in a more romantic way than she thought of him.

"Dominic . . ." Jennie squeezed his hand and kissed his cheek, trying to keep things light. "I'm going in now. I'm totally wiped out. Besides, we've got a plane to catch tomorrow."

Dominic stood, then took her hand and pressed it to his lips. "Of course. Good-night, señorita. I too must get some rest."

She'd done it again. Triggered something in Dominic that closed him up. She turned and hurried inside, up the staircase and into her room. Maybe when things settled down she'd talk to Gram about him. He seemed troubled by so many things. And she cared about Dominic. She really did.

Jennie crawled into bed, exhausted. Outside of her room, water bubbled in the fountain and cascaded over the rocks in the garden. It should have calmed her, but it didn't. The water served only as a grim reminder that she was stranded in a foreign country, while the ship, which carried her family and a DEA agent named Roberts, was drifting farther and farther away.

18

The next morning after breakfast Maria and Manuel García hugged them and offered their prayers for a safe journey. His uncle handed Dominic the keys to one of his private planes and ordered a driver to take them to the airport.

Jennie could feel trouble stirring deep in the pit of her stomach. Maybe it was the tearful way Maria had said goodbye, or Señor García's concerned expression when he gave Dominic the keys to the airplane. Dominic had assured her he knew how to fly. Was that it? Was she just being paranoid about getting in a small plane with a guy she barely knew? Or was there something else? Her intuition had been sending so many warning signals lately her brain was beginning to short circuit.

"Trust your instincts," Gram had often told her. Jennie's instincts told her she should be on board the *Caribbean Dreamer*, but it was a little late for that. The next best option available to her at the moment was to fly to Georgetown with Dominic. She'd have felt a lot better about it though if she could read Dominic's mind.

Dominic had been unusually silent during breakfast. Pensive. Maybe he was having second thoughts about flying her to Grand Cayman. Maybe he was just upset about her comments last night.

Now, sitting in the back of one of Señor García's limousines, Jennie glanced over at Dominic and smiled. "Thank you for everything you've done. I really enjoyed meeting Maria and your uncle Manny. I'm almost glad I missed the boat."

Dominic nodded. "They are nice people."

"You seem upset about something."

"Do I, querida?" Dominic paused, then frowned. "Forgive me . . . I think you do not like for me to call you my beloved."

"I didn't say that, but you're right. I don't mean to hurt your feelings, but the term seems so . . ."

"Affectionate?" Dominic took her hand in his and pressed it to his lips. "Perhaps you are right. It is too soon. I do not mean to offend you." His face brightened. "And today we will have a great adventure. I have much to show you before . . ." Dominic paused. A shadow crossed his face.

"You don't have to fly me to Georgetown, you know," Jennie offered. "I could probably get a commercial flight."

Dominic shook his head. "No, señorita. It is nothing. I would like to take you. We will get there much more quickly in Tío Manny's plane."

He was right about that. Two hours later they were circling a beautiful Caribbean Island. Jennie decided she'd been silly to worry. Dominic was an excellent pilot and flying in the small craft made her want to take lessons—maybe even get her own plane someday. Maybe Gram would teach her.

Jennie studied the island, looking for the airport.

"Um, Dominic, I hate to say this, but are you sure this is Grand Cayman? I mean, it can't be. There's no city, no resorts."

The island on which Dominic was preparing to land consisted largely of jungle and patches of open fields. Just ahead of them lay a crude landing strip, six planes on the ground, and a large hangar. A dozen or so trucks that looked like military issue had been parked off to one side of the runway. On the far side of the island, Jennie noticed a long sand spit with a marina at one end. The sun glinted off the metal roofs of a dozen or so metal structures. And on a hill, overlooking it all, stood a castle.

The landing gear dropped into place. Jennie swallowed back her growing uneasiness.

"Where are we? Why are you landing here?"

"Do not be alarmed, Jennie. I wanted to surprise you. This is my grandfather's island."

Jennie gripped the leather seat to control her anger as much as to brace herself for the landing. "Trust me, Dominic, if you didn't want to alarm me, this was the wrong move. I can't believe you'd bring me here without asking me."

"You are right. Perhaps I did act foolishly. But I wanted you to meet my grandfather. I have arranged for the others to join us here tomorrow. Matt will bring them. You will be safe."

Dominic's lack of conviction when he said the word "safe" set off a wave of terror. What if Dominic had been the shooter? What if he wanted her dead? *No, McGrady*, her inner voice warned, *don't panic. Don't read any more into this than you can see on the surface. Dominic's family does things a little differently than you're used to. That's all.* He'd had plenty of opportunity to kill her, but he hadn't.

Dominic's a friend—eccentric maybe—but a friend. Give him some slack and see where it goes. And pray.

Not bad advice. Actually, other than screaming her guts out there wasn't much else she could do—at least not at the moment.

"You will love our island, Jennie. The hacienda is more beautiful than Tío Manny's resort. I hope you will relax and enjoy it."

"You're sure you talked to Gram?"

"Matt is making all the arrangements. You will see."

Dominic eased the plane onto the landing strip like a veteran pilot. That should have made her feel better. It didn't.

Jennie did not like being manipulated. She did not want to be here. What was Dominic thinking? What did he want? They were friends. One minute they were having a great time on Jamaica, then poof, everything went wrong. She still couldn't believe it. Arrested for smuggling drugs she knew nothing about. Dominic had bribed the guards and they'd set her free—no charges or anything. Now she was on an isolated private island in the Caribbean with a guy she'd known for less than a week.

It was all too bizarre to be a coincidence. Had Dominic been planning this little side trip all along? No, that wasn't possible. He couldn't have known she'd miss the boat . . . unless he had been the one to set her up. Had he planted the cocaine and devised this elaborate plan to get her here? Why? What possible reason could he have?

McGrady, back off. You're letting your imagination run ahead of your common sense. He likes you and took advantage of the opportunity to show you his world. It's that simple. A private island. A gorgeous guy with money to burn. Enjoy it.

With no other choice available, Jennie followed Dominic to a waiting Jeep. "I am sorry I could not offer you a more pleasant ride to the hacienda, but the roads . . ." he shrugged. "You will understand when you see." He helped her into the passenger seat and climbed in the other side.

They bumped along a narrow, unpaved road that wound through the jungle. There may have been room for two vehicles to pass, but Jennie doubted it.

Even though she'd told herself to relax, she couldn't. As they drove along, Jennie tried to scope out the island in case she needed to escape. "It must be difficult to be so isolated. Is this the only road to the airport?"

"Sí. My grandfather is what you call . . . a recluse. The island is a fortress. It is heavily guarded to assure his privacy. The only other way is by boat."

A camouflaged truck with an open bed, like those she'd seen at the airport, came to a stop in front of them. Dominic pulled off the road to let it pass. The driver, a large surly man wearing a sombrero, nodded at Dominic and flashed him a toothy grin. Another similar truck followed. Both were laden with bulging burlap bags. And guarded by four armed men in combat fatigues.

Drugs. The word slammed into her stomach and nearly tore her insides apart. She closed her eyes and clung to the roll bar above her head. *Oh God, no. It can't be true. Please don't let it be true.*

Jennie gulped back the question she couldn't ask and pretended only a passing interest in what she'd just seen.

"Are they heading for the airport?"

"Sí. Grandfather exports coffee beans, both from Colombia and from here." He glanced over at her. "You noticed the guards. That concerns you, no?"

Jennie hauled in a deep breath to fight the rising hysteria. "Concerned? Why should I be concerned?" Her voice had shifted to soprano. "You bring me to your island, and the first thing I see are trucks loaded with *coffee* transported by armed guards."

"Perhaps they are just hitching a ride to the airport. We have many employees and they often go to visit their families on the mainland. We are not more than twenty-five miles from Cozumel."

The thought gave Jennie hope on two fronts. One, that drugs were not involved, and two, they were not as isolated as she had first thought.

The road widened. Mud gave way to concrete and the jungle disappeared behind them. The buildings Jennie had seen from the air were massive up close. They drove through what looked like a loading area. Several men were tossing bundles from a large storage bin onto a truck.

"The coffee beans are brought here from the fields," Dominic said, confirming her thoughts. "From here they go either to the airport or to the docks. Occasionally we have customers who ship by sea."

Dominic turned away from the workmen and pulled into a parking lot that held several other Jeeps. All the same camouflage colors. If Jennie hadn't known better, she'd have suspected she was touring a military compound.

Military. Maybe not drugs, McGrady. Maybe guns. Smuggling guns to . . . someone. Was that good or bad? Jennie wished she'd paid a little more attention to the military goings on in Central and South America. She knew there were uprisings and rebel groups but had no idea what they were called or what they stood for. Maybe Dominic's grandfather was one of the good guys, supplying guns to troops who had pledged their lives to bring freedom to the oppressed. It sounded good. And it was much easier to accept than anything else she'd imagined.

"Welcome, my friend—to the hacienda of Juan Carlos Ramirez." Dominic stopped the Jeep and hurried around to her side. He had parked near a high stone wall topped with lethal-looking razor wire. The effect was softened slightly by remnants of the jungle that had either been planted or had survived the ravages of construction.

She scrambled out of the Jeep and took Dominic's proffered hand. They walked along the wall a short distance and stopped at a wide iron gate. Dominic punched a number into the small electronic box, and after a series of beeps, the lock clicked and the gate shuddered open.

Jennie hesitated. The temptation to run licked at the corners of her brain. She glanced back at the sea, cool and inviting, and counted the boats. Two outboard motors, a yacht, and a sailboat. Maybe she could reach one of them. *And maybe you'd better forget it.* Bolting now didn't make much sense. Dominic could outrun her. And even if she made it, the men, who looked more like desperados in a wild west movie than coffee-bean pickers, would gun her down before she got ten feet. All this went through her mind in less than a second, but Dominic picked up on her reluctance. Fortunately, he'd read her wrong.

"The sea draws you, querida? Does it not?" He took both of her hands in his and drew her forward as he backed through the gate. "It draws me as well. But come. Have lunch with me and meet my grandfather. Then I promise to take you sailing this afternoon."

Sailing. Yes. He sounded so normal, Jennie wondered if all the warnings in her mind were figments of her fertile imagination. He'd called her querida again. His darling.

Maybe the danger wasn't in the drugs, or guns, or armed guards; maybe the danger was in Dominic himself. Did he love her more than he cared to admit? Was he so overcome with passion for her that he'd abduct her? Had he brought her here to. . . ? *Don't even think it. Dominic's not like that.* The notion was so absurd Jennie nearly choked on her suppressed giggle.

No. She had to stop imagining things and look at the reality of what was happening. "That sounds wonderful, Dominic. So does lunch. I'm starved." Sailing. Being on a sailboat would give her an advantage. If need be, she could bop Dominic on the head and sail to the mainland.

Lunch consisted of fresh fruit, a wonderfully spicy shrimp burrito, and salad. The hacienda was cool, and Jennie felt certain she had never seen a more beautiful home in her life. Like Señor García's resort, there was an open feel to the main part of the house. The white stucco walls and large open windows added to its sense of airiness. Plants hung everywhere. At least in the living and dining area. The bedrooms were a different matter.

Her room—actually it was a suite with a bedroom, sitting room, and bath—overlooked the water. She loved it except for one small detail. The windows were barred. Jennie tried not to think about that, concentrating instead on eating and on their coming sail.

"You are enjoying your meal?"

"Very much so. I'm sorry your grandfather couldn't join us."

"He is in Cozumel on business for the day. You will meet him tonight at dinner. Like Tío Manny, Grandfather insists that our meals be taken formally, in the dining room. You still have the dresses Maria gave you?"

Jennie nodded. Maria had insisted she keep them.

The knots in her stomach tightened as Dominic spoke of his grandfather. She envisioned the bust in the Garcías' resort—stern, cruel, unbending. She wasn't looking forward to meeting him.

———

As promised, Dominic took her sailing after they'd eaten. Wearing a bright orange life jacket over her royal blue swimsuit, Jennie positioned herself on the bow and let the wind whip through her hair. She wished the wind could blow away all the unnecessary stuff that had collected in her mind over the last few weeks. The confusion. The lies. The questions. "I just want to be able to see the truth in all of this," she whispered.

Jennie turned and made her way along the starboard side toward the stern. She smiled, pleased that she'd remembered what to call the right side of the boat.

"Coming about!" Dominic shouted.

She knew what it meant—sort of—but it didn't register until too late. She caught a movement off to her left. The boom and mainsail whipped toward her. She ducked . . . but not soon enough. The boom caught her alongside the head and sent her hurling off the starboard into the sea.

19

Darkness shifted to gray. The cry of a gull drew her out of the abyss. Jennie licked her lips. They tasted salty.

"Please, Jennie. You must wake up. I could not bear it if you were to die."

She was on the boat, in Dominic's arms. Her head rested against his chest. Consciousness brought back the memory of the boom connecting with her head, and the pain. She reached up to touch the sore spot on her head and winced.

"Querida, you are awake."

"What happened?"

"I tried to warn you as the boat came about. Didn't you hear me?"

Jennie nodded. "Yes, but it took me a second to remember what you meant. By then it was too late."

"I am so sorry. I should not have expected you to remember."

Touched by his sincerity and obvious distress, Jennie turned to look up at him. "Dominic, it's okay. You rescued me and I'm fine. That's what counts."

He gazed at her for a moment, then closed his eyes. His jaw tightened. Jennie had the strangest sensation that his sorrow went far beyond what had just happened. Had the thought of losing her triggered memories of his father's death?

She twisted around to a more comfortable position. They sat quietly, floating on the water for a long time. Offering comfort without words. She could feel the bond between them grow stronger and more secure. It was almost a tangible thing, and Jennie wondered how she could feel so strongly about a guy yet not be in love with him.

She'd never known anyone like Dominic. Sensitive, so emotionally honest that at times she wanted to cut and run. Maybe that was it. She was fairly certain the feelings they had for each other would never go beyond friendship, but the ties that drew them together were so strong it frightened her.

Dominic drew away first. He cleared his throat. He'd been crying. "It is time we return to the villa. There is something I must see to."

When they docked, Dominic escorted Jennie as far as her room. He kissed her cheek saying he'd see her at dinner, then went toward his own room at the end of the long hallway.

That suited Jennie just fine. As usual, being with Dominic made her feel as if she'd come off a four-hour drive in rush-hour traffic. Jennie recovered a book from her beach bag, then found a jar of bubble bath and poured about half of it in the bathtub.

As the warm water washed away the dried sea salt, it also soothed her fears. Dominic hadn't brought her here to hurt her. He'd saved her life. His motives in bringing her to the island were probably as he'd said, to show her his beautiful home and introduce her to his grandfather.

So how do you explain the armed men running around in camouflage outfits? Ramirez has a small army on this island.

158

Normal people don't have armies to keep people out—or to keep their guests in.

"Forget it," she said aloud to dispel the anxiety building in her stomach again. "Just shut up and relax, McGrady. You think too much." She picked up her latest mystery novel and began to read.

———

At a quarter to eight Jennie closed the door to her room and made her way down the winding staircase into the living room. An angry voice came from somewhere in the back of the house. Señor Ramirez? The man sounded as rigid as Dominic had depicted him in his sculpture. Another voice, Dominic's, responded. They were speaking Spanish and Jennie had no idea what they were arguing about. Maybe Dominic was finally standing up for himself.

Then she heard the name McGrady and stiffened. Were they arguing about her? Before she could form any kind of scenario, the door to Señor Ramirez's office opened. Dominic appeared first. His eyes widened when he saw her.

The look she saw in them startled her. Was he trying to tell her something? Dominic came toward her and, with all the formality of a prince in court, bowed and kissed her hand. "Jennie, you are early. No matter. I would like to introduce you to my grandfather, Señor Juan Carlos Ramirez. Grandfather, this is my good friend Jennie McGrady."

"Señorita McGrady. My grandson has told me a great deal about you." Ramirez nodded his head and smiled broadly as he extended his arm. "Allow me to escort you to dinner."

Jennie swallowed back the hostility she felt for the man and forced herself to comply. She placed her hand on his arm and fell in beside him. Dominic walked behind. Ramirez pulled out a chair and held it for her, then seated himself at the head of the table. Dominic took the chair opposite her. Juan Carlos Ramirez picked up a small bell and rang it.

Mrs. Rodriguez, the maid she'd met during lunch, appeared with salads and freshly baked bread. Through a delicious dinner of roast lamb with mint sauce, boiled red potatoes, tiny asparagus, and glazed fried plantains, Dominic and Juan Carlos chatted with her and asked questions about her home and family.

Señor Ramirez seemed so warm and friendly he might have put her at ease. Yet even his gracious smile couldn't erase the traces of hostility that periodically crept into his voice and his face.

Mrs. Rodriquez brought in crepe suzettes for dessert. Jennie took a bite and exclaimed in appreciation.

"I am pleased you find Consuela's cooking to your satisfaction." Ramirez set down his fork and leaned back in his chair. "I understand your father disappeared a few years ago. You have not heard from him in all these years?"

Jennie's head snapped up. She froze, mouth open, fork poised a few inches from it. How did he know about her father? Had she told Dominic? Maybe. She couldn't remember. Even so, why would Dominic say anything? "No, we haven't," Jennie replied, carefully phrasing her response. "We were told that he died when his plane crashed five years ago."

"But you believe he is still alive, is that not correct?"

The hairs on her head and the back of her neck stiffened. He couldn't have known unless . . . the television show. *Easy, McGrady, don't panic. Stay calm and find out how he knows so much and why he cares.* She moved the fork holding a bite of crepe into her mouth. *Set the fork down. Chew. Swallow.*

She glanced at Dominic, hoping for an answer, support, hope, anything. He held her gaze for an instant, then looked away.

Jennie drew in a deep breath to steady herself. She had nothing to lose by being direct. "I used to believe my father was alive. But I'm curious. How did you know?"

His mouth widened into a wry grin. He placed his napkin on his plate and stood. "Perhaps I will let my grandson tell you that, señorita." His smile faded as he turned to Dominic and spoke in Spanish.

Dominic stood, hands clenched. His nostrils flared and for a moment, Jennie thought he was going to hit the old man. Ramirez's voice dropped to a hoarse whisper, and even though she couldn't understand the words, she felt the threat behind them.

"Sí. I will do as you wish." Dominic melted in the heat of the patriarch's fire.

Ramirez nodded and walked back into his office.

Dominic tipped his head back as if saying a prayer, and crossed himself. By the time he faced her, the look of anguish had almost left his face.

This is not a safe place, McGrady. Juan Carlos Ramirez is a dangerous man. Jennie hadn't a clue as to how she'd make it happen, but she had to find a way off the island.

"Dominic, this is making me very nervous. What's going on?"

"Un momento, querida." Dominic took her hand and led her from the house into the courtyard and through the gates, which now stood open. He didn't stop until he reached the sandy beach beyond the wharf.

His steps slowed. "It was not meant to be like this."

"I don't understand."

"It began when I saw you on television. You said you were searching for your father. At first I felt compassion for you." His grip tightened on her hand. "Then they showed the photograph. I could not believe it. I was looking into the face of the man who killed my father."

"The man who killed my father." His words turned Jennie to stone. Her muscles refused to move—her lungs to breathe. "I . . ." she stammered. "No. You must be mistaken. My father wouldn't kill anyone."

"Your father was working with the Drug Enforcement Administration. We knew him as Rafael Chavez. He and a number of other agents had infiltrated Grandfather's drug operation in Colombia. My father and I arrived only moments before they raided the compound. He tried to stop the man arresting Grandfather and was shot. I will never forget his face. That man was your father. We searched for him, and a few days later received word that he had been killed in another drug raid.

"I did not believe this. And when I saw his photograph I knew. I told my grandfather."

"No, you're wrong." Jennie wrenched her hand from Dominic's and ran. Reality crowded in on her like monsters in a nightmare. And she had let them out. She slipped in the loose sand and fell to her knees. What was it Roberts had said? Dad had made enemies. By appearing on television she had joined the enemy ranks.

"Oh, God, what am I going to do?" She drew in a shuddering breath. *Be strong. You have to be strong. They still don't know that Dad is alive. Maybe you can . . . Can what, McGrady? Pull off a miracle?*

Dominic hunkered down beside her. "It will do no good to run, querida. You cannot escape."

Maybe she couldn't get away, but at least she could get some answers. "It was you, wasn't it?" she asked with much more confidence than she felt. "You're the one who broke into my house back in Portland, and then locked me in the sauna on the ship."

Dominic reached into his shirt pocket and retrieved the stolen picture. "I had to be certain it was you."

"What about the spear? That was you too?"

"Sí." Dominic kneeled down beside her and took both of her hands in his. She tried to pull away, but he held fast. "Grandfather ordered me to kill you. Remember when I told you about my father and how I would avenge his death?"

"Yes. I told you revenge wasn't the answer. It still isn't."

"And you are right. I tried two times to kill you, but I could not. I am an excellent marksman. I ask myself, how can I miss such an easy target? And now I know. How could I kill someone I love?"

"Dominic, I still don't . . ." No, this wasn't the time to tell him he had a warped idea of love. "If you decided not to kill me, why did you bring me here? Your grandfather hates me. He's going to kill me, isn't he? You couldn't do it yourself, so you brought me here so someone else could?" Jennie scrambled to her feet and began walking back to the villa.

"No." Dominic grabbed her arm and swung her around to face him. "I will not let him harm you. He has promised to let you go."

"Then why am I here?"

"Forgive me, querida, but I had no other choice. Grandfather said if I could not kill you, then I must bring you to the island."

"Why?"

"He is using you to lure your father to the island. When Jason McGrady learns that Juan Carlos Ramirez is holding you captive, he will come to rescue you. Then he will be executed."

20

Jennie paced the floor of the room in which she'd been sequestered. Dominic had long since dropped her off and gone to bed. She'd waited until midnight to attempt an escape. The door had been locked from the outside.

She tried to hate Dominic for bringing her here, but couldn't. Dominic was a victim of his grandfather's anger and a patriarchal culture that forced him to comply with his grandfather's wishes—even when they were morally wrong. She only hoped that in the end Dominic would be strong enough to stand up for what he believed in.

She tried to hate Juan Carlos Ramirez. He was an evil man, a drug lord—a murderer. But hating Ramirez wouldn't solve anything. *Neither will berating yourself, McGrady.* True, but if she hadn't been so insistent—if she hadn't gone to *Missing in America* for help—none of this would have happened.

On the ship, Roberts had warned her to be careful. How could she have been so stupid? She should have been able to see what was happening. She had even suspected Dominic at first. But in the end, Dominic's plan had gone off without a hitch. He'd gained everyone's trust—timed everything just right. Had his uncle and aunt known? Did Señor Ramirez rule their hearts as well?

She stopped at the window, slid open the glass, and pressed her face against the bars. "Oh, Daddy," she whispered. "I'm so sorry. I only wanted to know the truth about you. I found it. You really are alive. But for how long?" She sighed and walked back to the bed. "Don't come for me, Dad. Whatever you do, don't come."

He would. She knew it and so did Ramirez. If Dad really was alive, he'd come.

Jennie crawled into bed, fully expecting to be awake all night. She curled into a ball, closed her eyes, and prayed.

———

Bright sunlight and the distant fluttering of helicopter blades roused her out of a deep sleep. It took a moment for her brain to assemble the shattering events of the last few days. When it did, she bolted upright and ran to the window. The bars served as a grim reminder of her imprisonment there.

A helicopter could mean Dad had come to her rescue. Her hopes dissolved as the chopper set down on a pad just beyond the warehouse and two men in camouflage uniforms stepped out. It was too far away to tell who they were—only that they were Ramirez's men.

Jennie had never felt so helpless in her life. Part of her wanted to crawl back into bed and never get out. Part of her, probably the McGrady in her, had no intention of giving up. There had to be something she could do— some way to get off the island and find help. And she'd better hurry; it was already after nine.

With renewed determination, Jennie showered and dressed in one of the short sets Maria had given her. This time when she tried the door it opened.

Surprisingly, her appetite hadn't been diminished by Ramirez and his plans. Breakfast smelled wonderful. In the dining room, Jennie discovered a buffet table spread with fruits, juices, milk, scrambled eggs, salsa, toast, and hash browns with diced red and green peppers.

Jennie took a plate and helped herself, passing up the salsa and the peppers.

Judging from the food left in the serving dishes, the others had already eaten. That suited Jennie just fine. With any luck at all, she'd be able to avoid Ramirez and Dominic all day. Maybe she'd wander around outside and look for a way to escape.

She took her plate out to a patio off the dining room and sat down on one of the wrought-iron benches. Flower beds bordered a wide expanse of red Spanish tile. A set of stairs led to more gardens and a wide grassy area that sloped to the edge of a cliff.

She'd seen the cliff from the other side during her sail with Dominic the day before. It dropped off and fell about thirty feet to a rocky shore. A person could get seriously hurt if they chose that route—unless they had a rope and something to fasten it to. *And you have about as much hope of getting a rope in this place as you have of making it snow.*

Voices from inside the villa drew her attention. From where she sat she had a view of the living room and the door to Señor Ramirez's office. Ramirez emerged and two men followed. Probably the same two that had disembarked the helicopter earlier. This time Jennie had no trouble identifying them: Matt Hansen and "agent" Brett Roberts.

The food Jennie had just eaten threatened to make an exit the same way it had gone down. She turned away, hoping Ramirez hadn't seen her—wishing she hadn't seen

167

them. *Maybe it's not what you think, McGrady. Roberts may not be one of them.* Jennie took several deep breaths and concentrated on keeping her food down. Roberts was an agent. He knew her dad. He'd pushed her down when Dominic had shot at her. Had he found out about Ramirez from Matt? Was Matt an agent too?

Or were they both working for Ramirez? She could believe it of Matt—sort of—but Roberts? She'd trusted him. Had Roberts been acting as an agent to get information from her? She'd been deceived so often and by so many people, Jennie didn't know what to think or whom to believe anymore.

"Ah, there you are." Ramirez had seen her. "Señorita McGrady. I see you have made yourself at home." He eyed her empty plate. "That is good. I want you to be comfortable while you are here." He turned and motioned toward Matt and Roberts. "Gentlemen. I believe you have met our guest?"

Neither of them answered. They may as well have been cast in stone. She could read absolutely nothing on their faces to indicate which side they were on. Roberts adjusted his sunglasses and folded his arms, looking more like a hit man than a federal agent.

Undaunted by their lack of response, Ramirez continued. "Mr. Roberts, as you know, works with the DEA."

How had he known that? Had Roberts been caught trying to rescue her? No, he looked too cool and put together.

"Don't look so surprised, señorita," Ramirez crooned. "I'm certain that even as young as you are, you are aware of certain agents who, how shall we say, are willing to make deals? For a price, we were able to persuade Señor Roberts to deliver a message to your father.

Señor McGrady should arrive this afternoon. When he comes I will arrange for a small family reunion. Then, señorita, at sunrise tomorrow, he will be executed."

So that was how he knew Dad was alive. If Jennie's mouth hadn't been so dry she would have spit on Roberts. "You traitor. I trusted you."

Matt grabbed her arm and pulled her back. "Let go of me." Pain coursed through her shoulder when she tried to twist away.

"What do you want us to do with her?" Matt asked, tightening his grip.

"Leave her." Ramirez was apparently tired of tormenting her. He seemed to enjoy playing with people, driving them to the edge.

"You're not going to get away with this. My grandmother is going to know I'm missing. She'll send the police."

"I think not, señorita. Señor Roberts has assured your family that you are enjoying your stay so much you will not be meeting them until they dock in Cozumel. By then it will be over."

He'd won another round. Jennie shrugged out of Matt's grasp when he loosened his hold, and she ran into the villa. She rounded the corner close to the stairs and nearly collided with Dominic, who was just coming down.

"Querida, what is it? What has upset you?" Dominic asked the question as if he honestly didn't know why she was upset. His dark eyes looked so innocent Jennie wondered if someone had suddenly changed scripts on her. But this was no movie. She sat down on the stairs and buried her face in her hands.

Dominic dropped down beside her. "It pains me to

see you so unhappy. What can I do to help?"

Jennie took a deep breath, forcing down the hysteria. She was coming close to the edge. Somehow, she had to hold on to the slim thread of sanity and common sense she had left. She had to find a way through it. She raised her head and met his gaze.

"If you really want to help me, then stop your grandfather. Don't let him kill my father."

Dominic lowered his head. "I cannot. Justice must be served. 'An eye for an eye.' You will be safe, querida. That is what matters."

"No. That's not what matters. What matters is that you can't just go around killing people. Shooting my dad isn't going to bring your father back. I don't know why it happened, but I do know Dad wouldn't shoot anyone without a reason. And more killing won't make it get better. It's wrong."

"I am sorry. I . . ." Dominic unfolded himself and stood erect.

Jennie bounced up and grabbed his arm. "Wait. Kill me instead."

"What are you saying?"

"You and Juan Carlos need to avenge your father's death. Before you decided my dad was alive, you were going to kill me, right? Well, do it. Kill me instead."

"I do not understand."

Jennie wasn't sure she understood either. All she knew was that she would do anything to save her father, even if it meant losing her own life. Something Roberts had said about Dad tumbled into her head and seemed to turn on the lights. "It has something to do with sacrifice. There's a verse in the Bible that says, 'There is no greater love than this, that a man would lay down his life for a friend.'

That's what it's all about, Dominic. Dad gave up his life with us so we could be safe. He sacrificed everything for his family and his country. I didn't really understand that until now."

Dominic stared at her for a moment, his dark eyes glistening with unshed tears. "Perhaps that is what happened with my father as well. He sacrificed his life to save my grandfather. You see, Juan Carlos had drawn a gun and your father was going to shoot him. My father stepped between them. Grandfather and I escaped."

"Dominic, you can't let him kill my dad."

Dominic shook his head. "It is too late. I cannot stop him." Jennie sank to the steps again and watched him walk away.

21

Now what? *Face it, McGrady, you are in big trouble here.* Jennie decided to follow the same course her mind had been taking earlier. Ramirez was letting her wander around freely. Apparently, he didn't feel she was a threat. That could work against him.

She walked back outside and took her time strolling through the gardens. If anyone were watching they'd think she was just admiring the flowers or going for a walk. When she reached the gate, she stopped to admire a bird of paradise, then walked on.

No one stopped her, so she headed toward the boat docks. Off to her left, several men tossed bags of coffee beans into a truck bed that had already been partially loaded. A dark plastic tarp covered another kind of cargo. Most likely cocaine. The drugs would be hauled through the jungle and transported to the States, where they would probably be sold to dealers and resold again to kids too dumb or in too much pain to say no. Jennie shook her head at the thought.

Ramirez was an animal. And Dominic? Even if he wasn't involved, he had to know about the drugs. Jennie tried to imagine what it would be like to be in Dominic's shoes. Would she stay loyal to her family at all costs? It wouldn't happen, of course—Jennie was certain of that—but *if* Gram or Dad broke the law, could she turn them in? It was a question she hoped she'd never have to answer.

Jennie tore her attention away from the warehouse and the trucks and concentrated on the water—her most likely means of escape. A couple of boats bobbed on the water about a mile off shore. She could swim that far. Were they Ramirez's men, or a way to freedom? She'd just have to chance it.

"If you're thinking about making a getaway, I'd reconsider."

Jennie spun around in the direction of Roberts's voice. "Did Ramirez send you out here to keep an eye on me?"

"Ramirez thinks you're a helpless female. I know better."

"Hummph."

"I'm going to get you out of here, but you're going to have to trust me."

Had she heard right? "You can't be serious. You turn my father over to that creep Ramirez, and now you want me to trust you?"

Roberts glanced behind him. "I *am* an agent. So is Matt. I took a break from my duties to help you through this business with your dad. I didn't realize until this morning that Matt had been assigned to Dominic as a way of getting into Ramirez's inner circle—or that Dominic was Ramirez's grandson.

"By the time we got word that you and Dominic were not on board the ship, you were already on your way here. About the same time I discovered who Matt was. He briefed me on Ramirez and his operation, and we decided to team up."

"You expect me to believe that? You're both agents,

both on the same ship, and you didn't know what was going on? Never mind. Let me guess. The fewer people who know, the better."

"That's right."

For some strange reason she believed him. "I think you guys need to change your policy."

"Maybe. But first I have to get you off the island. And we have to do it in a way that doesn't hinder the DEA's plan to take down Ramirez and his operation. The U.S. government has been after Ramirez for a long time. Caught up to him a couple of years ago in Colombia, but his son interfered and Ramirez slipped away from us. We managed to shut him down for a while, but he emerged bigger and more powerful than before."

"You're going to arrest him?"

"We're going to do more than that, Jennie. We hope to close him down for good. We don't want anything to go wrong this time."

"What about Dominic?"

"We'll just have to hope he has enough sense to stay out of the way while the bullets are flying and that he'll cooperate with us when it's over." Roberts glanced up at the villa and frowned. "Go back in the house, have lunch as usual and come back down to the docks at 1400 hours—two o'clock," he added for her benefit.

"I can't leave without Dominic."

"Impossible. He might tip off his grandfather. We can't take that chance."

"But . . ."

"Jennie, this is important. I don't have time to argue with you. Divers from those boats out there will be setting explosives at strategic points on the island. At exactly ten minutes after two we let 'er rip. Matt's men will raid the compound, and you and I will be on our way to Cozumel."

"Why are you telling me all this?"

"Because you need to know. If I'm going to get us out of here alive, you've got to do exactly what I tell you."

"What about my dad?" Jennie glanced up at him. "What's going to happen. . . ?"

Roberts removed his glasses and raised an arm to shade his face. "He'll be safe."

Their eyes met and Jennie's question stuck in her throat. Brett Roberts's eyes were the same dark blue as her own. Shock waves coursed through her. She felt as if she'd been trying to open a lock for years and suddenly the door had swung open.

Brett Roberts was her father. Older, balding, shorter than she remembered—but then she'd grown at least a foot since she'd last seen him.

Daddy. She opened her mouth to say the word aloud, but he held up his hand.

"Don't, Jennie." His eyes told her he wanted nothing better than to take her in his arms—to hold her and protect her like he had when she was little. But he didn't. He replaced his glasses and stepped away from her. "We'll talk about it later. You need to get back. Ramirez will wonder what we've been talking about."

Jennie wanted to throw her arms around him and hit him at the same time. Later they'd talk. Now she didn't dare make any move that might betray him to Ramirez. Slowly Jennie turned away, then headed back up the hill and through the gate. Her mind felt numb. Ramirez was walking toward them. *Careful, McGrady. If you slip up or show anything other than dislike for Roberts—Dad—Señor Ramirez might suspect.*

"It's bad enough you bring me here as bait to lure my father. But do you have to send your scummy friends to stand guard over me? You know there's no way for me to get off the island, so why don't you just leave me alone."

Beneath the scowl on Roberts's face, she could almost imagine him cheering her on. Or maybe he was warning her not to overact. Jennie flounced past the old man and went inside. She made it as far as her bedroom before her knees collapsed.

She fell back onto her bed, unable to believe it. Dad was here. Roberts. How could she have missed it? No wonder she had trusted him. On some level she must have known all along.

Dad was actually here. And they thought he was one of them. What a coup.

Jennie wanted to spread her good news to the entire world. "Thank you, God. Thank you, thank you, thank you. Dad's getting me out of this place and everything's going to be all right."

Jennie bolted upright. *No. Not everything. Not Dominic*. Dominic wouldn't hide, or cooperate. His strong sense of family would bring him running to protect his grandfather, just like his father had. If she could warn him, maybe he'd be able to get away, but knowing Dominic, she doubted he'd run. Besides, she couldn't risk saying anything to anyone. Blowing Matt or Dad's cover at this point could not only mess up their plans to get Ramirez. If she wasn't careful, she could get them all killed.

Still, McGrady, you have to find a way to protect him.

During lunch, which she and Dominic shared with Matt, Roberts, and two other men, Jennie put her plan into motion. "Dominic, this waiting is driving me crazy.

176

How about taking me sailing this afternoon?" She glanced at her watch. "Say in about half an hour?"

"You are sure, señorita? After yesterday, I am not certain you trust me."

"What happened yesterday," she paused for emphasis, wanting to make certain her father didn't miss her meaning, "was an accident. You saved my life. Please, Dominic. I'd really like to go sailing."

After obtaining his grandfather's permission, Dominic agreed, and at five minutes to two they met in the living room. "Un momento, querida," Dominic said as he headed back to the stairs. "I have forgotten something. A gift for you."

"Can't it wait?" Jennie called after him, but he'd already gone. She glanced at her watch. Four minutes. *Come on, Dominic. Hurry.*

Three minutes. Dominic joined her. She grabbed his hand and hurried out of the hacienda and into the courtyard.

When they reached the iron gate, Dominic stopped and pulled her up short. "I know you are anxious to go, but first you must listen. I have been thinking about what you said to me. It was wrong of me to bring you here and endanger your life and your father's. My grandfather . . ." Dominic shook his head. "He is wrong to do this." Dominic took Jennie's hand and pressed a heart-shaped gold locket into her palm, then closed her hand and raised it to his lips. "For you, querida. I give you my heart."

"Oh, Dominic. It's beautiful." Jennie swallowed hard. One minute. When this was over she'd give it back. She had to get him down to the boat. She slipped the locket around her neck, took his hand again, and drew him forward. "This will make our sail even more special."

"No." He pulled his hand out of her grasp and handed her a key. "I am not coming with you. The motorboat at the end of the dock. Take it and go to the mainland. There is danger here. I have learned that Grandfather does not mean to let you go."

"Dominic, it's okay."

"Please, listen to me. I will do what I can to help your father. I promise. Only now you must go."

Two o'clock. Jennie glanced in the direction of the dock. *Think, McGrady. You've got to get Dominic down there.* "All right. I'll go, but . . . come with me to the boat. If I go alone, your grandfather's men might stop me. Please, Dominic."

To Jennie's relief, he agreed.

When they reached the dock, Jennie glanced around. Where was Dad? Great. Now what? He could have been on any one of the five boats harbored there. "Dominic." She fingered the locket. "I wish you'd come with me. My father can take care of himself— that is if he even comes."

"No, I cannot."

Jennie handed him back the key. "Okay, but at least show me how to run this thing."

Dominic stepped up to the console and slipped the key into the ignition. As he did, Matt appeared behind him and touched his neck. Dominic went limp.

"What are you. . . ?" Jennie stared as Matt caught Dominic under the arms.

"Get on board. Now."

Jennie obeyed. "What did you do to him?"

"Pressure point," Matt grunted as he dragged Dominic into the cabin, dropped him onto a bunk, and cuffed him. "He'll come around soon."

"Where's Roberts?"

"I don't know. He should have been here ten minutes ago. If he doesn't show in two minutes, you're going to have to take this thing out yourself."

"No, I can't . . . Roberts . . ."

"Something must have happened in there. He was talking to Ramirez. Look, if he doesn't show, get this tub out of here. Head west. You'll hit the mainland. If we don't connect, hand Dominic over to the federales. They'll know what to do."

Jennie tried to listen. *Oh, God, no. Not now. I just found him. Don't let anything happen.*

"Jennie!" Matt grabbed her shoulders. "Did you hear me?"

Jennie choked back the panic washing over her and nodded. Matt twisted the key. The engine roared to life. "Take the wheel. I've set it in reverse. Just back out, swing her around, and push the throttle forward as far as it will go." Matt jumped off the boat and gave it a shove. "Move it. Now!"

Jennie closed her mind to everything except getting the boat and Dominic away from the island before Matt and his men opened fire. She concentrated. *Back up, turn the wheel—not too much.* "God, please let my dad be okay." *Straighten it out. Good.* Jennie shoved the throttle forward. The boat leapt out of the water. The force threw her against the safety rail. She fell, jerking the wheel to the right. Jennie regained her balance and turned the wheel back. Too little, too late. The powerboat was heading straight for the cliff beneath the villa.

22

An explosion ripped the cliff apart, spewing rocks a hundred feet in the air.

Jennie pulled back the throttle and cranked the wheel to the left. As the boat straightened, she braced herself, opened the throttle, and raced toward the open sea. Every few seconds another bomb went off. The staccato sounds of gunfire raced to fill the silent spaces.

When she felt she'd gone a safe distance, Jennie swung the craft around, then idled the engines. The gunfire and bombs had stopped. Smoke billowed around the island, making it look like a volcanic eruption. She wondered how anyone could have survived.

The scene blurred. Jennie didn't bother to brush away the tears. *Dad. Don't even think it. He's okay. He just has to be.* She turned away from the wheel and sank onto a cushioned seat. In a few minutes she'd regain her composure and head west, like Matt had told her. Maybe she'd turn Dominic over to the federales. Maybe she wouldn't. It seemed a better choice to call his uncle Manny.

She heard a moan from the cabin and hurried below to investigate. "Dominic? Are you all right?"

He shook his head as if trying to orient himself. "What happened?"

"Matt put you out of commission for a few minutes. He's an agent." She hurried to his side. "Oh, Dominic. I couldn't let you stay on the island. When Roberts—he's an agent too—told me what they were going to do I had to get you out of there. I was afraid you'd be killed."

Still stunned, Dominic struggled to sit up. "What about Juan Carlos?"

"I don't know."

He glanced at his cuffed wrists, then raised his gaze to hers. "You must take me to Cozumel. I have much to tell the policía."

Jennie offered him an approving smile and lifted the locket from her neck. "You'll want this back."

"No, querida—my friend." He reached up to stop her and took both of her hands in his. "You must keep it. You have given me back my life. I can never repay you. So, please. The locket is so little a token for so great a gift."

Jennie blinked back her tears and nodded, accepting Dominic's gift and the kiss he left on her cheek. She drew in a ragged breath and stood. "We'd better go."

They went topside. Dominic stared at the island for a long agonizing moment, then tore his gaze away.

"I'm so sorry, Dominic. It was a beautiful island."

"It will be again some day," he said, looking back at the smoke rising from it. "Perhaps I will ask Tío Manny to build a resort there. And I will sculpt and paint again." He smiled at her. "Perhaps I will take your grandmother's advice and have a showing in the United States. You would come?"

"You can bet on it."

Dominic nodded and ducked back into the cabin, saying he needed to be alone. Jennie didn't ask why.

"From ashes to roses," she whispered, remembering one of her mother's favorite Bible verses. Dominic would be all right.

Jennie took the wheel. *But will you? Will Dad?* Matt had told her to keep going—to take Dominic to the mainland. But how could she leave Dad or Matt? They could be hurt.

Jennie pressed the throttle forward. Maybe she'd go a little closer. Have a look around. No. She shouldn't. Matt had given her orders. And going back could create more problems. Jennie aimed the boat toward Cozumel and eased the throttle forward.

She'd gone only a few yards when she noticed a powerboat heading toward them. Had Ramirez gotten away? Jennie held her breath and let it out again when she recognized the driver and the man who stood on the deck waving.

Matt slowed as he came alongside her craft. Roberts jumped onto the deck behind her. His lip was split and bleeding and he had a bruise on his left cheek.

"How's Dominic?" Matt asked.

Roberts ducked into the cabin. Less than a minute later his head and Dominic's popped back through the opening. "He's okay. Anxious to see his grandfather."

"Bring him aboard," Matt called.

Dominic still looked dazed as he let himself be transferred to the other boat. The transfer completed, Roberts gave Matt's boat a shove and waved. "See you in Cozumel."

Matt grinned and nodded. "Have a good trip."

Jennie and Roberts watched the boat fade to a small spot on the horizon. "Well, kid," he ruffled her hair. "We'd better head in too. Gram and J.B. and that red-headed cousin of yours will be anxious to see you."

"They're in Cozumel?"

"Safe and sound. I saw them and your journalist friend Hendricks just before Matt and I came to the island."

"Is Hendricks still on our case?"

"Nope. Matt gave him an exclusive on the Ramirez story."

"Do Gram and J.B. know?" she asked, hopping onto the bench seat to the left of the controls.

"Only that I'm an agent who used to work with Jason." Roberts took the wheel and swung the boat around until the prow pointed toward the late afternoon sun, then inched the throttle forward.

"Let me guess," Jennie said. "They didn't need to know so you didn't tell them."

"Right. As far as they're concerned, you fell into the hands of a notorious drug lord. Agents Matt Hansen and Brett Roberts were sent to rescue you. Had a dickens of a time convincing your Gram to stay put. She insisted on coming with us. Thought for a while we'd have to lock her up."

"What changed her mind?"

He shrugged. "I'm not sure. She was arguing like a she-bear protecting her cub. All of a sudden she backed off. Guess you'll have to ask her."

Had Gram recognized him too? Jennie couldn't wait to ask her. Yes, she could. There'd be plenty of time to talk to Gram later. Right now she wanted to concentrate on Dad and make the most of their precious few minutes together.

"What happened to your face?" she asked. What she really wanted to ask was: *Are you coming home?* She didn't.

She already knew the answer.

Roberts touched his cheek and winced. "Ramirez decided he didn't trust me. Sent a couple of his thugs to work me over.

Fortunately, the gunfire distracted them. I got the jump on 'em."

"Is he still alive?"

"Barely. Don't know if he'll make it, but even if he does, he'll spend the rest of his life in prison."

"What's going to happen to Dominic?"

"He'll be questioned."

"He won't go to prison, will he?"

"You gonna press charges?"

"Not a chance. He helped me get away. And he plans to tell the police what he knows."

"You're quite a girl, Jennie." Roberts wrapped an arm around her shoulder and gave her a hug. "Even if you do ask a lot of questions."

Jennie grinned so wide she thought her face would break. *You're going to have to give him up, you know,* a voice in her head broke through the happiness. Jennie sighed.

"Did you say something?"

"No. I was just thinking." Soon they'd be in Cozumel. She'd rendezvous with Gram and the others and finish out the cruise. Dad would go back to being an agent, fighting crime, and doing whatever else agents do.

"I can't go back, Jennie."

"I know." She'd lose him again, but for now, God had given them a little snatch of time and Jennie planned to enjoy every second of it. When it was over she'd store the memories in her heart and treasure them forever. "Will you change your identity again?"

"Probably."

"Will you contact me from time to time?"

"If I can." He grinned down at her, tears glistening in his eyes. "You take good care of Nick for me, ya hear? And don't be too hard on Michael. I hear he's one of the good guys."

Jennie choked back her tears. "Sure."

"Roberts?" she said when she was able to speak again. "Tell Dad I love him." Jennie wasn't sure why she'd gone back to thinking of him as Roberts. Maybe she just wanted him to know that his secret was safe with her. Or maybe she was just now beginning to understand what he'd been trying to tell her all along.

Roberts nodded. "Your dad said to tell you he loves you too."

They went on talking about family, friends, and Jennie's future. And she did have a future—not like she'd planned. But it was looking pretty good just the same.

Jason McGrady was gone forever. *But,* Jennie reminded herself, *Brett Roberts, or whatever his new name will be, is very much alive and maybe—just maybe when the danger is past— you'll see him again.* Jennie watched him for a while, then leaned her head against his shoulder and committed him to memory.